THE DIPLOMATIC SPY

Welcome to clever illusion and cold-hearted treachery

Shawn Callon

Love is whatever you can still betray. Betrayal can only happen if you love.

John Le Carré, A Perfect Spy

Operatives (spies), as well as agents, typically fall into three groups – the idealists, the money hungry and the afraid.

The Diplomatic Spy

Walter Talbot, CIA Head of Station, Paris

DEDICATION

This novel is dedicated to the many brave citizens of Eastern Europe who were a part of the Peaceful Revolution that led to the fall of the Berlin Wall on November 9th 1989.

ACKNOWLEDGMENTS

Cari Redondo from A Work of Heart by Cari for her careful formatting of my manuscript for publication.

My spouse Elizabeth for her tireless work editing my manuscript.

PROLOGUE

A fter graduating from High School in the USA Simon decided to visit Europe for a year or so in order to improve his language skills, get an understanding of European culture and of course find a way to pay for his living expenses. If he could save some cash, all the better.

In 1989 all of Europe was excited by the anti-communist Demonstrations taking place throughout Eastern Germany and the whole Eastern European Bloc. Simon was working construction on sites in Southern France near Chamonix. The enthusiasm and fearlessness of the German protesters impressed him so much that he persuaded two of his co-workers in Chamonix - a fellow-American, Walter Talbot, and John French from the UK- to take a short vacation in Berlin to help take the Wall down.

Both of his friends remember him saying with great passion "We know how to destroy and build walls so let's travel to Berlin, rent a truck and load up with sledgehammers, pickaxes and chisels. We can then help bring down one of the worst symbols of Soviet Communism. The West did nothing to help the East Germans when they rebelled in 1953, or the Hungarians in 1956 or the Czechs in

1

1968. We can do our bit now. What do you say?" Both Walter and John were up for an adventure like this and they all took off for Berlin in late October 1989. Unfortunately for Simon this well-intentioned undertaking left him with a crippled and withered left hand until 2020.

Before Simon persuaded his friends to go on this ill-fated trip to Berlin, he had already spent the first six months of his European exploits in Spain. He had served drinks in hotels, given private lessons in English, worked construction as a general laborer and had held down other temporary jobs traveling from Bilbao to Madrid to the Island of Mallorca. His Spanish was perfect.

Being somewhat interested in art, he had taken full advantage of his free time in Spain to explore many galleries and museums that stored national and international treasuries that had been donated, bought or stolen over many centuries. He had visited one of the largest and richest Spanish museums outside Madrid, the Bilbao Fine Arts Museum. It houses a valuable and very comprehensive collection of Basque, Spanish and European art from the Middle Ages to contemporary times, including paintings by old masters together with 19th century and modern artists. But when he moved onto Madrid and visited the Prado Museum, Simon could have spent days and days delighting in the many thousands of drawings, paintings, prints and sculptures that the museum had acquired since its inception in 1819.

Asked which artists impressed him the most and why, he might have replied "that's a really tough question. I'm not an artist but as they say I know what I like. Well, there are three artists whom I really like and respect – I wish I had their visual talents. Velázquez, El Greco and Dali are up there in my estimation. All three of them had a lasting effect on art many, many years after their deaths."

"Velázquez's portraits although painted during the 17th. Century Baroque period have an eternal quality about them that move me.

His art went on to influence the early Impressionist and modern day artists some 200 hundred years later. Next would come El Greco. His idiosyncratic and individual style fascinates me but unfortunately it was not properly appreciated by his contemporaries. Somewhat like Velázquez his talents transcended the centuries and helped give birth to the Expressionist and Cubist movements of the early 20th. Century. And lastly I would include Dali. I just love the illogical complexity of his surrealistic creations, he in some ways reminds me of El Greco."

His reply may sound slightly pompous but here was a young man who was clearly affected by his exposure to the world of art and was struggling to articulate why.

Finishing his Iberian experience on the beautiful and unspoiled island of Mallorca, Simon decided to move to the Chamonix area in France. Although one of the oldest winter resorts in France, Chamonix is a stunningly beautiful area for summer visitors as well. And as luck would have it, Chamonix urgently needed construction workers. The three friends worked hard and played hard. Walter was tall, very laid-back and always had a new girlfriend; John was the shy one – bookish, loved to go for long walks alone in the Alps and would come back to share the most amazing photos of Alpine scenery he had taken with his Zeiss camera. He was a nature-lover and he would sit for hours describing in fine detail all the flora and fauna he had discovered on his walks. Folks who met Simon's two friends would easily remember them – the tall American Casanova and the naturalist Brit. With Simon it was different. He was of average height, of average build, with average looks – almost forgettable. However, all the heavy outdoor work he had been doing while working on construction sites had toned and tanned his physique giving him a very self-confident attitude and a determined demeanor.

What was really memorable about Simon though was his skill with language. He was fluent in English (of course), French, German and

Spanish. His mother was a very accomplished character actor able to adapt to many different roles and accents during her theatrical career in the USA. He had clearly inherited her linguistic skills. His father was a professional magician whose sophisticated maneuvers had wowed many audiences throughout the US and Europe – Montfort Sr. was truly a master of deception and illusion. Simon wasn't quite sure whether he had inherited this skill but time would tell.

MAJOR CHARACTERS

Simon Montfort, Cultural Attaché, US Embassy Republic of France

Béatrice Montfort, Simon's spouse, musician

Suzanne Montfort, their daughter, fashion designer

Phillippe Montfort, their son, student

Guy Dubois de Prisque, Béatrice's brother, transplant surgeon

Walter Talbot, Simon's friend and CIA Head of Station, Paris.

Mary Talbot, his spouse

John French, Simon's friend and former member of UK Customs & Excise

Amira Takács, Simon's former Hungarian girlfriend

Harold J. Schwarzkopf, US Ambassador, Republic of France

Daphne Schwarzkopf, his spouse

Charles Heyworth, Charge d'Affaires, US Embassy Republic of France

Anna Heyworth, his spouse

Justin Heyworth, their son

Stephanie, Simon's assistant

Eric Haupt, Simon's assistant

Mehmet, Simon's Turkish agent

Antonin, Simon's Bulgarian agent

Hans, Simon's Austrian agent

Joseph Erdész, Simon's Hungarian agent

Erzsébet Erdész, Joseph's daughter

Mickey, Joseph's associate

Alexei, Simon's Russian agent

Natasha, his spouse

Argun & Shali, Chechen Moslem activists

Fontaine family, hold the loan on Heyworth's home

Ian Churchill-Davidson, Orthopedic Surgeon, British Military Hospital, Berlin

Elizabeth French, John French's spouse and former nurse at BMH Berlin

Alice Montfort, Simon's sister in USA, archeologist

Ivan Ivanovich, President of the Russian Federation

Steve Gannon, POTUS

Roy Shoore, VPOTUS

Senator Pius, Chair of the Senate Purity Committee

Marc Renaud, Montfort family attorney

Andrew Weiss, Chargé d'Affaires, US Embassy, Republic of Hungary

Istvan Ferenczy, Amira's spouse, Head of Internal Security, Hungary

Karik Petrov, Istvan's Head of Security

'Blago' and 'Toma' Serbian paramilitary police officers

1 AMERICAN HOSPITAL OF PARIS, NOVEMBER 2020

Mumbling drowsily, Simon struggled to move his arm in his bed "this doesn't feel like our king bed at all". His left hand was heavy and was throbbing like a jackhammer. His mouth felt like sandpaper. "How are you feeling?" a warm, disembodied female voice asked. "I don't know who you are and I can't see you and I'm feeling lousy" was Simon's tart reply.

"We'll give you some more medication and we'll talk later" said the voice.

"Will we?" And with that question hanging on his lips, Simon fell back to sleep.

Simon Montfort, Cultural Attaché at the US Embassy in Paris, was recovering from an eighteen hour operation to replace his crippled left hand. The operation involving thirty medical professionals took place at the American Hospital of Paris under the leadership of the renowned French reconstructive transplant surgeon Professor Guy Dubois de Prisque who happened to be Simon's brother-in-law. Simon's left hand and forearm had been mangled over 30 years ago as a result of an accident at the Berlin Wall in 1989.

While Simon was recovering from his major surgery in the American Hospital de Paris, his wife Béatrice was on the phone trying to find out from her brother Guy when she could visit her husband.

"Mon Dieu, Guy, will you stop talking to me like I am one of your students. I don't need to hear the details of Simon's operation, I just want to know when we can come to the hospital. So again, when can we see him?"

"I just want you to appreciate what he's been thru. He's been highly medicated because of the pain. Even when he's talking he's somewhat delirious. You can come and see him anytime. He may know who you are, he may not. I don't want you to be upset."

Guy was older than his sister Béatrice and despite his self-important exterior he was very protective of his younger sibling. Guy had chosen medicine as his career and had become a highly respected surgeon and academic in his chosen field of plastic surgery and high-risk transplants. Their parents had both passed away – Madame Dubois de Prisque had been a successful scientist and Monsieur had reached the pinnacle of his academic career as President of the Sorbonne University in Paris. Though both her parents wanted Béatrice to pursue a scientific career, she decided to follow her passion for music. She is an accomplished musician, arranger and composer and is well-known throughout Europe having previously played first violin for several years with the Orchestre de Paris.

As Béatrice and her two adult children (Phillipe and Suzanne) drove to the hospital, they talked about the long decision process Simon had gone thru and were worried about how he would react to his new hand. He had taken a long time thinking about the side effects of the anti-rejection drugs, how well the new hand/forearm would work and how good it would look. Guy had reassured him many times that since he was still a relatively young man of fifty in excellent physical condition he would make a strong recovery.

"That's good to know, Guy, but how good will it look? Will the pigment, skin tone, hair pattern and its overall size match my other hand? I don't want to walk around looking like some sort of freak."

"There are bound to be differences, Simon. We could be waiting another 10 or 20 years before we find an exact match. I will choose the best possible facsimile ensuring that the hand is from a white male of a similar age who has followed a similar lifestyle to you. You will have to trust me. I have done this operation before and they have all been very successful. And that means no complaints. You have to remember that there aren't that many good quality hands available. Most donated hands come from old people who have passed away or from unfortunates who have died in their prime years from illnesses or tragic accidents. Only a few are usable. The supply is very limited. The biggest issue for you will be physical and occupational therapy. The muscles and tendons in your left arm have had limited use the past thirty years, so you will have to spend a lot of time each day for many months strengthening them. Otherwise the new hand will be as useless as the one you have. "

Although fairly ineffectual, his crippled hand had given him a certain "rakish" aura. He rather enjoyed telling enquirers how and where the accident happened – "at the Berlin Wall in 1989, in fact at the AlexanderPlatz in the British Sector" etc. etc. He was a rather vain man careful about how he looked and about what he wore. One would think that he would have gone to great lengths to hide his crippled hand; but Simon was a man of many complications as we will find out. He rejected the idea of a prosthesis saying to Guy on several occasions "I don't want to look like a pirate sporting a hook instead of a hand". (He really wasn't interested in modern prosthetics and Guy had given up trying to educate him. Instead as a joke, Guy would present him with a range of hooks he had acquired from a theatrical props store and playing along with Simon's humor he would ask him to select his preference!)

Eventually Beatrice had grown tired of his indecision. "I appreciate this is a serious step you may be making Simon, but Guy has given you all the possible reassurances you could ask of a surgeon. I know my brother can be overbearing at times but he is a brilliant surgeon and I have complete faith in him. So please make up your mind and stop discussing it with us all the time. Our children, our friends, your colleagues at the Embassy and I think the operation is a good idea. But the final decision has to be yours."

So in November 2020 the day before the US Presidential Election, Simon was being prepped for surgery. Just before the anesthetic was administered, he made one last request of Guy before he became unconscious "please make sure that you attach my new hand the right way round". Guy replied with a serious face "I'll try to remember that, Simon. I'll do my best."

The day after the Election Béatrice and their two children were at Simon's bedside waiting for him to wake up from his latest round of meds. He looked well and was sleeping peacefully. The room was full of electronic medical equipment monitoring Simon's vitals; they made various beeping noises from time to time and occasionally the machines' LED's would flash different colors ostensibly giving some type of reassuring information to the attending staff. The room was pleasantly decorated in calming pastel shades and was full of cards, flowers and fresh fruit from friends and Embassy staff. Béatrice had requested that only visits from immediate family be allowed for the first few days after his operation. Once they had settled down in chairs round Simon's bed, the attending nurse told them some good news – "we have been able to reduce the potency of the narcotics and he will be waking very soon."

Suddenly Simon's eyes opened and he appeared wide awake. "Bonjour everybody" he said jokingly. "How do you feel, mon chéri?" asked Béatrice hesitantly.

"I feel good. My left hand is throbbing a bit still. So who won?"

No problem with his memory, thought his family.

"Bad news, Simon. Steve Gannon and his running mate Roy Shoore won a landslide victory."

He groaned loudly "That's awful. They're going to be much worse than the current lot." And with that he closed his eyes and went back to sleep.

Simon's nurse made an excellent recommendation "Give Monsieur Montfort an hour or so to rest some more. Why don't you take a light dinner in our cafeteria? The cuisine is excellent and inexpensive. He will be wide awake when you return." They took the nurse's advice and thanked her for taking care of Simon so well. "Je vous en prie" (you're welcome) she replied with a smile.

Before we move ahead with our story, it might be helpful to explain why Simon was appointed Cultural Attaché as historically the post has often been filled by writers and artists giving them a steady income and allowing them to develop their own creative work, while promoting their own country's culture abroad. Or the post was typically filled by Intelligence Officers needing diplomatic cover for their covert activities.

Simon fell into neither category. While Simon had an earnest passion for art and loved to read about the lives of famous painters, he could not paint or draw. Also he was not a member of an Intelligence agency and at the time had no interest in such a clandestine career. So he would seem at first sight as an unsuitable candidate for a Cultural Attaché position.

However luckily for him the US Department of State was so impressed by his flair for languages and by his achievements in the cultural affairs office while he was working in the US Embassy in the UK that they decided to promote him at an early age and at his request agreed to transfer him to the US Embassy in France as the Attaché.

2 US PRESIDENTIAL ELECTION 2020

The USA was in upheaval politically and economically. Inflation and unemployment had been rising since late 2019. So many students and small businesses had defaulted on their loan repayments that several large banks had gone under causing the economy as a whole to weaken. Consumer and business confidence had dropped. A repeat of the collapse of the US economy like 2008 was being forecast. People were worried and angry. The government did not know what to do. The President was being impeached and some senior members of his Cabinet and White House team were on trial for obstruction of justice.

In an attempt to deflect people's anger about these economic issues and to assuage the growing discontent of fundamentalist Christians, the Federal Government with the backing of the Supreme Court had passed stringent legislation affecting voting rights and women's reproductive rights.

These new laws stipulated that voters had to show a valid US Passport or an original birth certificate or original naturalization documents in order to vote; because of claims of widespread voter fraud, regular ID would no longer be acceptable. The new law allowed individual States to reduce the number of polling stations in non-white districts and increase the number in white districts; the use of absentee ballots was prohibited except for members of the military. Lastly all felons were banned for life from voting in any election.

Many Christian organizations were also very pleased when a new law banning all forms of birth control except for the rhythm method was passed by a narrow margin in both Houses of Congress. The legislation detailed the penalties for the sale, distribution and use of condoms, birth control pills and devices.

Violent anti-government and pro-government clashes broke out on university campuses, union halls and congressional district offices in urban and rural communities throughout the nation. Hundreds of people were arrested and sentenced to jail or prison depending on the severity of the crime. The two major political parties were in disarray. The Right was accusing the Left of fomenting disorder and the Left was accusing the Right of outright incompetence and rabid discrimination.

There was total political upheaval. The Republican Party had split into three separate groups – the ultra-right Liberty Party, the right-wing America First Party and the traditional Republicans. A group calling themselves New Progressives had spun off from the Democrats and had formed their own left-leaning Party. The result of the National Election result was a landslide victory for the America First Party led by Steve Gannon and Roy Shoore. Their party won 61 seats in the Senate and 259 seats in the House. The traditional Republicans and Democrats had been virtually eliminated from Congress as the remaining seats in Congress had been won by the New Progressives. The divide in American politics had become much worse, reflecting what had been happening in society.

A major tenet of the America First Party's manifesto was the creation of a committee to investigate the religious and moral purity of all Federal and State employees. Gannon and Shoore were adamant that "our economic decline is being caused by our dwindling attendance at church, our reluctance to obey God's Truth in the Ten Commandments and also by the immoral pursuits of adultery, gambling, substance abuse and financial corruption. Our Party promises to clean up America and we pledge to start with investigating all government employees on day one of our Administration. Any employee from the most senior to the lowest will be terminated without any compensation if he or she is found to be offending our principles of religious and moral purity. "

They promised that new legislation would be passed to enable the creation of Purity Courts in all counties throughout the USA to investigate the behavior of all state, county and city employees. The criteria for deciding whether an adult was leading a morally pure life would be written by a secret committee of political leaders appointed by Steve Gannon. (It was announced later that Senator Pius would chair the Purity Committee. He was a well-known expert in identifying moral contradictions since he had been a personal friend of Bernie Madoff, the 21st. Century's wizard of lies and fraud.)

The names Gannon and Shoore may sound familiar. Gannon used to be a member of the previous Administration but had been terminated in 2017; Shoore used to be a State Judge but had been fired for his unlawful religious activities as a judge and for his alleged predilection for under-age girls.

Many Federal and State employees were shaking in their shoes worried about what the government committees might know already, what their colleagues might say about them during committee hearings and what secrets their families might find out as all hearings would be live streamed.

Meanwhile the beleaguered current President issued a combative statement thru social media – "My name will be cleared. My impeachment is a farce made up by the fake news media, the deep State and a bunch of mean-minded congressmen. It's so sad to see our country in such turmoil, the likes of which we have never seen before. We shall see what happens under President Gannon. But I will tell you this – if I could've run again I would've won again bigly and there would be peace and harmony in our country. Believe me! God Bless America!"

The leader of the New Progressives issued a statement as follows "with the humiliation of the President's impeachment and the prosecution of a good number of his Cabinet, we should be proud that our institutions did the people's work. But now a large and ominous shadow has been cast over our great country. The election of Gannon and Shoore symbolizes the twin evils of political tyranny and religious hypocrisy. We have no idea what will happen over the next four years but my fellow Progressives and I will continue to fight for every citizen's civil rights and to continue to protect our Institutions from the evils of supremacist tyranny."

3 US EMBASSY PARIS NOVEMBER 2020

While Simon was recovering in hospital and enduring his physical therapy, big changes were happening at the Embassy. The current Ambassador had resigned immediately after the election of Steve Gannon. His replacement was the current American Ambassador to the UK Harold J. Schwarzkopf Jr. He had been appointed pro tem Ambassador to France pending Senate approval after the Inauguration. This was most unusual as the Chargé d'Affaires would normally assume the Ambassadorial responsibilities until Senate confirmation.

Harold was a large and colorful individual devoid of most diplomatic skills and intolerant of international protocols. He had however a strong streak of natural cunning and had proven business abilities. He had been plucked from the oil fields of the world by the current President and had been appointed to the prestigious position of US Ambassador to the UK. His nickname was "Dirty Harry" – mainly due to his association with the black gold that had made him a billionaire but also due to the rumors about his sexual adventures with young female embassy staff, in fact any young women that he could lay his hands on. It is reported that to avoid some rather salacious lawsuits he had made several large financial payments thru shell companies over the years. These amounts had been dispersed to various "young women" who had agreed to keep their mouths shut. While in the UK he had managed to keep his hands and other body parts to himself. However, the ladies of France might prove too tempting for him!

Simon heard about these changes when the Chargé d'Affaires, Charles Heyworth, came to visit him. The Chargé and he had a good relationship both within the Embassy and socially. They and their wives had dinners together and enjoyed each other's company at the theatre and at concerts.

"This is not a good week. First we have Gannon and Shoore and now we have Dirty Harry. What a great advertisement for our country – a wannabe Nazi and two alleged sexual predators! It's unbelievable! What's next?"

"Don't get too excited. You need to get better so you can return to the Embassy as soon as possible" said Charles. "How well do you know the new Ambassador?"

"I've met him a couple of times when I visited London to discuss bi-lateral cultural projects with my opposite number over there. Dirty Harry's quite rough but very intelligent. You think he's not listening to you but he's actually taking everything on board. Most of the UK Embassy staff will be delighted to see the back of him, though. Unfortunately he is the archetypal ugly American abroad. He hasn't done much to improve the "special relationship" with the Brits. I can't see him encouraging much "entente cordiale" while he's in France. Soon you and I will face a dilemma."

"What dilemma?"

"Do we help him to be successful or do we undermine him?"

"What on earth do you mean, Simon?"

"Oh, don't worry. Put it down to my meds. Let's talk about something else."

Charles Heyworth was a career diplomat having spent close to 30 years in the Foreign Service. He was a small man with sharp features and a quick mind but he was very cautious in thought and deed. The very idea of undermining the new Ambassador was an anathema. He was used to Simon blurting out provocative ideas thinking that Simon did this sometimes to see where people stood while keeping his own views to himself until a more opportune moment for sharing arose. But on this occasion Charles believed that Simon was serious.

"So how is the new hand going?" asked Charles.

"Quite good. Can't do much with it though. I'll be moving to a rehab facility tomorrow for intense therapy, I guess that means painful. I'll be there a week and then home where I am told I need to carry on with the therapy for another six weeks. I'll be back at the Embassy in just over a week. So how do you feel about the way that Dirty Harry was appointed? Typically you should have been made Ambassador pro-tem."

Charles demurred a while before answering. "I don't care Simon. I'm drawing to the end of my career in the Service. To be honest I never wanted the top job. I don't mind standing in now and again but it's so political. The President says this, his Secretary of State says that, the WH Press Room says something else. You can't get clarity on anything nowadays."

"Ah, that's what makes it so much fun, Charles. When those around you and above don't have a clue, you can stake out a claim and go for it."

"That might work for you, Simon, but not for me. I'm counting the days until my retirement. Then I can return back to the US, pick up a couple of directorships of companies, do some non-profit work and grow my orchids."

"And then die of boredom?' replied Simon with a faint smile. "By the way Béatrice will be here soon, you can stay if you like. She likes talking with you."

"I should be leaving as I have to get back to the Embassy for a meeting with our new leader. Is he going to visit you in hospital?"

"He had better hurry up as I'm leaving here tomorrow."

"Au revoir Simon."

"A bientôt Charles."

As Charles left he saw Béatrice walking gracefully along the hospital corridor. He had always admired Simon's wife and stopped to chat with her for a few minutes. He assured her that Simon was doing well and then he hurried off for his meeting with Dirty Harry.

Béatrice entered Simon's room and asked tenderly "How is my patient doing today?" as she held his right hand.

"I'm feeling much better. What I'm excited about is getting all these bandages off and seeing what the new hand and forearm looks like. Guy says that will happen early tomorrow morning before I move to rehab."

"That sounds great. I'm sure you'll be pleased with the result. I am so glad you will only be staying in rehab for a week and then you can home so I can look after you. I have cleared my diary for the next month while you recover at home."

"That's too bad because after rehab I'm going back to work at the Embassy."

"I know that's what you intended but Guy insists that you need to take extreme care and recommends at least one month of observation in case you experience any side effects to the anti-rejection drugs. Also Suzanne and Phillipe want to spend some time with you."

"That could be a problem. I have a new boss, Dirty Harry from the UK. You remember I mentioned him to you?"

"How could I forget your colorful description, mon amour?"

"I need to meet up with him at the earliest possible moment. I don't want to see him at a rehab facility and I'm certainly in no hurry to have him come to our home so soon. We will have to invite him and his spouse eventually, mon chéri, but it can wait."

"What is so important about cultural affairs that you have to meet him while you're still recovering?"

"Nothing" Simon replied brusquely. In a more mollified tone he explained "there are some serious issues at the Embassy that he needs to be aware of. Stuff I cannot reveal to you right now. That's all."

"Can't someone else handle this? You have two very capable officers – you are always praising Stephanie and Eric saying what excellent work they do, how reliable they are."

"It's nothing to do with cultural affairs. I came across some important information recently that I need to share with the Ambassador face-to-face. Don't worry. I'll take care of it."

Béatrice had learnt not to probe too much when Simon was in this sort of mood so she let it go for now.

4 NEW US AMBASSADOR

Against the advice of Guy and Béatrice, Simon asked to meet Ambassador Schwarzkopf briefly at the Embassy before his week of rehab. His wife was furious. Simon's response was "it can't be helped". The good news was that his new hand and forearm were an excellent match so he didn't look like a freak. Béatrice drove him to the Embassy telling him again that he was unfit to be having a meeting with the Ambassador. She left him at the security gates and said she would be back in an hour to take him to rehab.

The US Embassy in Paris is the oldest diplomatic mission of the United States. It is located at 2 Avenue Gabriel on the northwest corner of the Place de la Concorde, which was the site of many notable public executions of royalty during the French Revolution.

The Ambassador and Simon agreed to meet in the Embassy's private conference room since it was protected from any external surveillance or cyber-attack. It was always swept for electronic bugs prior to any conversation. The Embassy staff were surprised to see Simon back so soon. "Just here for a quick meeting with the Ambassador and then I'm leaving again for a week."

Without exception the staff told him he would need all his diplomatic strength for any meeting with Harold as *"he's being a demanding pain in the"* ***" and *"disrupting the work of the Embassy"*. He stepped into his office to chat with his two officers, Stephanie and Eric, and was annoyed to find out that Harry had directed them to change many of the arrangements they had been making to promote American culture in France.

"I don't want to see any more paintings that no-one understands, any more sculpture that looks vulgar, any more orchestras that play foreign music. Do you understand? I want to promote old-fashioned, wholesome American values. I want to see works of art featuring eagles soaring high in the sky, Mickey Mouse movies, Ronald Reagan's speeches, songs of Sinatra, sculptures of Hulk Hogan and so on. I want to impress our French friends with our strength, our patriotism, our determination. That's the message our new President wants to convey. I need your new plan on my desk in a week."

Simon was staggered by what he heard. He said he would get back to them after his meeting with Harry.

"Ah Si, good to meet you again. Hope that operation won't hinder your work here. I don't understand why you need to have so much time off."

"Thanks for the welcome, Mr. Ambassador. Allow me to congratulate you on your appointment here. I guess you have never had transplant surgery. Anyhow I need to run the reports that I have recently received from some my agents past you so you're up-to-date and also share my concerns about the direction you gave to my staff."

"Call me Harry. I sure haven't had any operations like that. All my body parts are in excellent working order. Anyway enough of getting to know each other. Down to business."

Harry made sure he continued with his agenda showing little, if any, interest in Simon's news and concerns. "The President Elect has instructed me along with all the other Ambassadors that we immediately cease all activities against Russia and its allies. I know your network has done some outstanding work over the past years that has embarrassed the Russian President and his East European spy networks, but we must stop. We are going to reset the relationship big time. The day after the Inauguration the two Presidents are going to sign a new comprehensive agreement covering trade, defense and security. At the same time the White House will be announcing that we are leaving NATO as a gesture of goodwill to our Russian colleagues. You will need to roll up your network immediately and cease all activities. Is that clear?"

Simon replied "Please call me Simon. I hear what you're saying, Harry."

"You don't like being called Si? Strange! Anyway, we are going to change our focus. The target is International Islamic Fundamentalism. All Sunni Muslims in Europe and Russia will be subject to surveillance. If they so much as fart or drop one piece of trash, they will be detained and interrogated. Got that? The Americans, the Russians and the Europeans are going to rid the world of this blight once and for all. My directive is that you will set up a new network to infiltrate Sunni Moslem groups suspected of plotting terrorism. I want your plan of action on my desk within the week."

"That could be a problem. I'm in rehab for the next week to make my new hand and forearm work properly. I'll do what I can. I must leave now as the pain has just returned." (It hadn't but Simon couldn't believe what he was being told and had to leave before he exploded.)

"That's not going to be good enough, Si sorry Simon. If you still want your job when you get back you better make sure that I have that plan otherwise you and your lovely family will be on a slow boat back to the good 'ole US of A!"

With that Simon excused himself and exited the room. The only pain he was feeling was *'a pain in the **s'* from his meeting with Harry. He couldn't share his fury as only three people knew about his real work at the Embassy – the Ambassador, the prior Ambassador and the Head of Station in Paris, Walter Talbot. He phoned Béatrice careful to keep his voice calm and asked her to return as soon as possible.

5 REHAB

On their way to rehab, Béatrice could see that Simon was agitated. "That was a very quick meeting. What happened? You don't look at all happy."

"Dirty Harry was his usual boorish self. He wants me to change all my priorities and come up with a new plan. The President-Elect is going to make some big policy changes that will be announced in January. I'm bored already. Let's talk about your concert engagements."

"That's not like you, Simon. Something's going on. What big changes do you have to make to your cultural programs? Surely they can't be that dramatic?"

"I wouldn't say they are dramatic but they will take a lot of rework. I have got a week or two to sort it all out. No problem. When are you leaving for Rome?"

"Next Tuesday for two weeks unless you prefer me to put it back for another week or so?"

"No, you go. I know you want to be with the Orchestre de Paris for

Daniel Welding's last performance before he stands down as Conductor. I wish I could be there in Santa Cecilia Hall and see you play and listen to the wonderful acoustics of that place. Please be careful of your hearing. I read somewhere that a lot more symphonic musicians have to wear earplugs nowadays or use Plexiglas screens to avoid damaging their hearing. They are four times more likely to experience hearing loss than the general population."

Beatrice's hearing had been affected by years of sitting in an orchestra surrounded by the loud music of her companions. She had decided that her appearance as First Violin with Daniel Welding would be her last. To avoid further damage to her hearing, she had decided to concentrate more on composing her own original pieces and also arranging classical works. She had not revealed this decision to Simon yet. She was sure it wouldn't be a problem. All he wanted for her was her happiness.

"I will take care but I'm not going to wear ear defenders or use those ugly plastic screens. I need to hear the music and need to be seen as a part of the orchestra. But this is going to be my last live performance, Simon. I want to move onto other creative avenues while I am still young enough."

"I'm pleased. You are going to compose and arrange?"

"How did you know?"

"Philippe mentioned it to me."

"Il est trop bavard."

"No he's not too talkative. We were discussing hearing loss and he said you ought to quit orchestral concerts as he's concerned about your hearing."

"Simon, here's the rehab facility. It looks like a fancy hotel. Are you sure it's not?"

"Well let's see if we can find any folks in white coats or black scrubs, shall we?"

The residential facility was located on the very upscale Avenue Montaigne in the 8th. Arondissement. It was called the Dubois Clinic for Advanced Physical Rehabilitation and was owned by Beatrice's brother, Guy. It looked like a hotel on the inside. There were no white coats or black scrubs; instead lots of well-dressed, young and fit looking staff were talking with guests (patients) about the services of the clinic.

Simon announced himself at reception and was told that Guy would be down to see him in a few minutes. As he waited he noticed a mobile phone store across the street. He needed to get a burner phone so he could call Walter Talbot. "I'll be back in a few minutes. I need to buy a new battery for my smartphone."

When he returned with both a new battery and the burner, Guy was chatting with his sister.

"Ready for your week of discomfort, Simon?"

"What type of battery did you get?" asked Béatrice suspiciously. She was convinced that somehow Simon was going to carry on performing his embassy duties while he was in rehab.

"This one" Simon replied showing her, "long life type, won't need charging for a week."

"Yes, I'm ready" replied Simon to a bemused Guy.

"We'll be starting in 30 minutes once you have checked into your room. You'd better say au revoir to each other." Turning to his sister, Guy advised "You can visit Simon in a few days. You'll be amazed at the flexibility and strength he will have achieved by then."

After kissing Béatrice goodbye, Simon went to his room. It was huge

– king size bed, big screen TV, balcony overlooking the busy Avenue Montaigne, wet bar, office desk, secure safe and a 5 Gigabyte wireless internet connection. Using his burner he left a coded voicemail for Walter at the CIA asking for a meeting at 10p that night at a pre-arranged location which had been coded as 'the corner of Rue Boissy d'Anglas and Rue du Faubourg Saint-Honoré'. There would no reply or acknowledgement.

Guy suggested they had a quick lunch at a local bar before rehab started. Simon chose his favorite course of confit de canard with pommes dauphinoise and ratatouille. Guy ordered grilled skinless chicken with walnut and beet salad followed by fresh fruits. He did not approve of Simon's choice saying "Make the most of this fatty meal, Simon, as you will be eating much healthier food at the clinic."

"How does that help my hand?"

"Let me explain the philosophy of my clinic and the intense seven day schedule of rehabilitation you are going to experience. Most physical therapy takes place over a period of weeks and maybe months consisting of sessions of 30 to 60 minutes two or three times a week. In cases like yours, Simon, we will intensify your treatment for maximum effect. You will get tired, your new hand will hurt but I guarantee you will appreciate the result. So that your body can get the full benefit of this type of intense therapy, you should follow a low-fat, low-glucose diet. We want your cardiovascular system working 100% unhindered by too much fat and sugar. By the end of your stay here, I will have your left hand making phone calls, tying your laces, typing on your keyboard, opening bottles of wine, driving a car again and so on. And even more important - caressing your beautiful wife."

"I'm ready, Guy. I have faith in you."

"Excellent. Your first session will start today at 1.30p and finish at 4.30p. You will have two rest periods lasting 30 minutes each. Once you've completed this first round of therapy, I suggest you have a light dinner in your room so you can relax. We will give some pain killers to enable you to sleep. If you need any help at all in your room, press the emergency button once and a medic will be with you within 2 minutes, night or day."

Guy escorted Simon to the treatment room and said he would see him later.

6 WALTER TALBOT

By the time 4.30p came around Simon was in agony. Too much bending, stretching, lifting, pulling, massaging – his left hand was throbbing. He returned to his room, ate a snack from the refrigerator and took two Tramadol for the pain. He was not sure how he could last until his 10p meeting with Walter. As he was going thru the TV channels, his room phone rang. He picked up and a pleasant voice said someone had hand-delivered an envelope for him. It was down at the front desk. Simon asked for it to be brought to his room. Thinking that it might be a change of plan from Walter (but he would have called him on his burner) he was surprised to see a postcard inside the envelope.

It was postmarked a few days ago in Chamonix, France. There was a brief note on the card and Simon recognized the photo immediately. The note read "ton coin préféré" which translated into "your favorite place". The lush, gentle sloping hills covered in vibrant Alpine flowers set against the snowy backdrop of Mont Blanc – that was the abiding memory Simon would always have of his time in Chamonix. The card was not signed but he knew the sender. Her name was Amira Takács. Originally from Hungary, she worked in

Chamonix at an upscale hotel as a conference translator. She was fluent in Hungarian, Russian, English and French. They had met at the hotel one evening when Simon was attending a conference on the "Rebirth of Democracy in Europe". She was assisting the Hungarian Trade Delegation and spotted Simon as he was looking at some of their printed handouts written in Hungarian. In perfect French she asked him "do you speak Hungarian?" "Not a word" he replied "but I like the way you speak French" he said with a twinkle in his eye. She blushed and responded "Your French is very good too and I detect a slight American accent. I have an older sister, Mari, who lives in the States. Where are you from?" From that brief exchange a relationship started to flourish. In retrospect Simon would always say "we were just good friends" but Amira's feelings went much deeper.

Simon wondered why Amira would be sending him such a postcard. They had not met or talked since they had separated in Berlin in 1989. And more to the point how did on earth did she know that he was at the Dubois Clinic? Pushing aside these questions, he had to refocus on his meeting with Walter. Simon had known him for over 30 years and they were firm friends. Simon had decided to join the Foreign Service and Walter had joined the CIA. John French had returned to the UK and had joined Customs and Excise working undercover a lot of the time. Because of the considerable discomfort from the therapy, Simon took a long shower to get some relief and made some subtle changes to his appearance "just in case" as Walter would say! The time was approaching 9.30p and Simon was feeling very tired and uncomfortable but he made his way to the rendezvous point. The street was bustling with Parisians and tourists and no-one appeared to be taking any notice of Simon – he was just too average. Even so, Simon followed his usual tradecraft to make sure he was not being followed. He stopped in front of the impressive window displays of the luxury store Lanvin and checked to see if anyone was hovering near him; then he crossed the street and doubled back once or twice to make sure nobody was tailing him; and lastly he turned down a few side streets and looked back to check. Typically it takes a team of six to follow a suspect without arousing suspicion. Simon was quite confident that he was alone and he arrived on time at the rendezvous where Walter was nonchalantly reading an advert for a 15% discount on sales of men's clothes. Simon nodded imperceptibly to him and passed him a short written message saying "meet me at Reynaud Bar opposite".

Walter looked very quizzical but crossed the street and walked slowly to the bar. The atmosphere on the terrace outside the bar was full of the pungent odor of Gauloises and Gitanes as it was illegal to smoke inside. They went straight to the bar and ordered two beers. Walter had heard about Simon's hand operation and immediately asked him about his recovery.

"It's going well but the therapy is like torture. But what is worse is the news I got from my new boss. We had better finish our beers and walk along Faubourg so we can chat in private."

Walter restarted the conversation saying "You are being very careful, Simon. What's with the burner? Don't you trust your own people? What's been happening? I've got some great news to share with you before you share yours. I received approval today from my Director to proceed with Operation Gotcha against the Russian President. The video that one of your agents obtained is pure gold, Simon. We checked the authenticity of the audio as well as the video and it's definitely the Russian President and it's his voice you can hear. The confession of the two guys who were with him naked in a bed and having gay sex only adds to its authenticity. No-one will believe that it's phony. It will be released clandestinely tomorrow thru social media. You have to be proud of the work your network did."

"Yes that's the problem. Harry has told me to roll up the network completely and set up a new organization to subvert the so-called Islamist threat. This order came from the top of the new

Administration. What have you heard?"

"That sounds dangerous. I've heard nothing like that. On the contrary my boss is delighted with the video and wants more incriminating evidence of the Russian's hypocrisy and corruption. But then who knows what is going to happen in a few months. As far as I'm concerned the video will be released unless I'm told otherwise. You will know from the media when it has happened. Perhaps Harry is jumping the gun or he could be following his own agenda. We shall see!"

"I don't trust Harry at all. He comes with a bad reputation. He's annoying most of the staff at the Embassy. That's why I'm using a burner. You had better delete the message I sent you setting up this meeting, Walter. Also I wouldn't put it past Harry to put a tail on me. You had better check to see if you are being followed."

"Don't worry about me, Simon. I deleted your message immediately and my phone is in a Faraday bag so no-one can track my location. Our meeting didn't happen, OK?"

They carried on walking reminiscing about old times and catching up about their families. They had another quick beer at a different bar making sure to pay cash and then took their separate ways. Simon took a different route back to the clinic, again making sure that he was not being tailed. He removed the SIM card from his burner, destroyed and threw it into a trash can. Even if someone had been following him and had recovered it from the trash, they would have been wasting their time as the SIM was useless.

"I wonder what the Russian President's anti-gay policy will be now" he mused to himself.

7 MOSCOW 1989

I n Chamonix Simon and Amira spent much of their free time walking in the warm, fresh mountain air talking about developments in Russia and Eastern Europe. The night before the weather had turned stormy very quickly as it can so easily do in the mountains. They were at Amira's hotel on the balcony under a canopy watching the power of the storm: one minute the mountain peaks were dark, merging with the threatening clouds and then suddenly when the lightning started the peaks looked as if they were on fire. Then the thunder rolled thru causing the canopy to shake, frightening them for a second and then making them laugh at their timidity. The rain poured down the canopy and flooded the street below. People ran madly to get away from the storm. They heard someone below laugh and say "il pleut comme une vache qui pisse" (it's raining like a pissing cow). Simon was captivated with the scene. He just kept staring at the mountains while he held Amira closely to him. He had never seen such a Son et Lumiere before in his life. If only he could paint the scene like one of the French Impressionists probably had done in the 19th. century.

They went for a walk the following morning. Again Simon could not help talking about the weather – it was crisp, it was cool, it was fresh. The rain was still dripping from the leaves and trees as they walked along the slick forest paths. "Simon, you are quite the poet. Have you thought about painting it as well?"

"I love art and I wish I could paint this scene but unfortunately I don't have that skill. All I can hope for is one day I will have enough wealth to own pieces of outstanding art that express scenes like this. But for now I'll settle for experiencing this exhilarating climate. Soon the sun will come out and everything will be dry again. I'd love to live here."

"They do have winter you know. Snow, avalanches, ice storms. You'd hate that."

"Yes, I would but I wish I could paint those scenes. Anyway, let's get going and I'll stop talking about art and the weather."

Simon really enjoyed Amira's company – she was intelligent, well-educated, attractive and, like Simon, interested in politics. She also had a quiet, shy sense of humor which he rarely found in American women.

They shared their backgrounds with each other. Amira's turned to be far harsher than Simon's easy life growing up in the US. He hadn't realized what life had been like for Hungarians under Communist rule. She explained that the 1956 Uprising had been ruthlessly put down by Russian tanks and military. No-one had come to the aid of the Hungarian people. In 1958 following the execution of Imri Nagy (the leader of the Uprising), some of her relatives escaped to the West. One of her unmarried great aunts fled to the UK where she was hired by the BBC World Service to broadcast news to Hungary. The Soviets soon worked out who she was and Amira's family was punished. Her father had been a faithful member of the Communist Party and had a well-paid career in the Budapest Workers' Council. He was fired from the Party for complicity with an agent of a foreign power (that is, his aunt) and he lost his job. To keep the family together he had to take a low-wage job sweeping the streets while Amira's mother had to earn money by taking in laundry from neighbors. Her parents lost their subsidized housing and utilities. Life was very hard. Many of their former friends ignored them. But fortunately for Amira a distant relative offered to help her. He paid for her education and helped her get a job as a translator with the Foreign Trade Department when she left school. Her older sister, Mari, was lucky as well. A few years ago she applied to join an exchange program to visit the USA for 6 months; she loved the American lifestyle so much she applied for permanent residency. "We have lost touch with each other unfortunately. She was always a little unstable back home so I don't know how she's doing."

"Oh Amira, your upbringing was really hard. I feel for you. My early life was nothing like yours. My elder sister, Alice, and I lived in a small Boston suburb. Although our parents were away a lot working at theaters and shows— my mother was an actor and my father was a magician – we had a happy childhood. Our parents would tell us such entertaining stories about people they had met or had worked with as they toured the East Coast. They would always make sure that one of them would stay at home while the other was touring.

Our father was always showing tricks to us as kids; our mother would suddenly break out into a character she had been playing or use a foreign accent to entertain us. We weren't rich and we weren't poor but we were all very happy. I can't comprehend what you went thru."

Amira suddenly collapsed into tears and buried her head into Simon's shoulder whispering "make love to me, Simon, make me happy."

So in the warm Alpine sun Simon lost his virginity, experiencing a physical and emotional happiness he had never felt before. They lay naked in the Alpine flowers saying very little but smiling at each other a lot and caressing each other's warm skin until it was time for both of them to return to work.

Simon returned to the construction site and mentioned to Walter what had happened. Like a big brother Walter responded "I hope you are using capotes anglais Simon".

"What are they?"

"Rubbers! You can get them at the drug store in the village. You have to prove that you are over 16. I would get down there as soon as you can. You don't want to get Amira pregnant."

"No, I don't. I like her a lot but I'm not ready for a long-term commitment."

The next time Simon met Amira, he asked her if she could teach him to speak Russian.

Pulling a very sad face Amira told him "Oh Simon, you don't know how much I hate that language. I had to learn it at school for years. Day in and day out we had to read Russian novels and recite revolutionary communist Russian poetry. I have tried to forget all my Russian but it is still there in my brain. It will never leave me. I am fluent in that language and will always be. I can teach you easily but it won't be enjoyable for me. But since it is you who is asking, we can start now if you like."

"Perhaps we can take a short visit to Moscow next month. I'll need a visa but I guess you can travel there easily."

"Why do you want to go there? Their regime is dying on its feet. The country is in a mess."

"But Secretary-General Gorbachev is talking about Glasnost and Perestroika (transparency and reconstruction), domestic reform, nuclear disarmament, social democracy – just think of it, Russia becoming a force for good in Europe instead an evil empire."

"Simon, you are wonderfully naïve. Russia will never become a liberal democracy. They fear the West too much –remember Napoleon and Hitler. Although these two empire builders were defeated by Russia and the Russian winter, they left a permanent mark on the psyche of Russia. The politicians in Russia will never, never trust the West and that means the USA. They hate NATO and they see the European Common Market (now called the EU) as a big threat. But I will be your tourist guide for a week if you want. I know Moscow well. You must be careful when we go there. The KGB and the GRU don't agree with Gorbachev's vision of a social democracy free from censorship and intimidation. So assume your hotel room will be bugged, assume you will be tailed to see what you get up to, assume that all of the currency dealers in the street are Soviet agents looking to get you arrested. Is that understood?"

"You make it sound so attractive. But yes I understand, Amira."

They booked a four day vacation in Moscow thru Intourist (Russian Travel Agency). They flew direct on Aeroflot on an Ilyushin 11-86 arriving at the Sheremetyevo International Airport in Moscow. The flight was uneventful save for the beverage service (no food was offered). The flight attendant pushed an old, noisy cart down the aisle offering large glasses of straight vodka, Russian brandy, Johnny Walker scotch – no ice and no mixers! Simon declined the hard liquor and asked for two sodas – "not available today" he was told.

"You will have to get used to shortages in Russia. Always plenty of liquor but no guarantee you can get anything else" Amira warned.

On their way to Hotel Ukraina (a Stalinist skyscraper built in 1957) their taxi passed many abandoned cars in the middle of the multi-lane highway.

"Why so many cars left in the road?" Simon asked in perfect Russian.

"They don't work anymore. Owners have to wait for new parts and then they will come back to their cars and fix them in the road" the driver replied. "It could be days or weeks. Depends on how much you can pay."

"Hey, what's that huge sculpture over there" Simon suddenly shouted.

"That's not a sculpture" barked the taxi driver. "They are tank traps. They commemorate the furthest point that the Nazis reached in 1941 during the Great Patriotic War. The Nazis slaughtered their way thru Poland, Belarus, Ukraine and then eastern Russia killing Slavs, Jews, Gypsies and Communists. We turned them back here under the brilliant leadership of Comrade General Zhukov, helped by the coldest of winters, temperatures fell to -49F. The Nazi war machine ground to a halt. My father and my uncles died in this spot."

"Can we stop and take a look?" asked Simon. Amira shook her head.

"Not today. We have to keep going. I am a busy driver, not a tourist guide."

They arrived at the towering Hotel Ukraina in the center of Moscow during one of the most beautiful summers Muscovites had experienced in the city for a long time. But everyone they saw looked miserable. Simon could not understand why. They checked in at the palatial front desk featuring Russian folk art on the wall behind the clerk and placed their documents on a most elegant counter made from the finest walnut. The clerk was wearing a name tag displaying his long first name but Simon found it almost impossible to read the name as the badge was hanging from the guy's shirt at an 'I don't care' angle. He finally gazed up and gave them a surly and unsmiling look – no "have a nice stay" here, Simon thought. He processed their documents slowly and eventually told them 'you can collect your papers in 48 hours after internal security has checked them'.

They had to hand carry their luggage to their room as the elevator "is not working today". When they reached the 7th. Floor they turned down the corridor towards their accommodation and Simon noticed an elderly Russian woman sitting on a stool knitting some sort of clothing. She sat very close to their room and was dressed in very old, dowdy clothes and wore a black headscarf. She didn't acknowledge either of them and just kept her head down concentrating on her work. 'Don't the old women in Russia sit at home and knit? Or are their apartments so cramped that they have to rent space in hotel corridors?' Simon thought to himself.

"What's with the old lady?" whispered Simon in case she understood English.

"I'll tell you later" responded Amira.

Their room was small and rather utilitarian but clean. The bed was approaching the end of its life. They managed to squeeze their possessions into the one small closet they found in the room. They read a notice by the phone informing them that if they wanted to make an international phone call, they would have to give 24hrs' notice and make sure they were sitting by their phone otherwise it would be cancelled! They then freshened up and talked about getting dinner. The hotel only provided breakfast so they would have to find a local restaurant. Returning to the front desk they found that the surly clerk had disappeared. Fortunately, a young smiling receptionist introduced herself as Nina and asked them whether they needed any help.

"Sure" said Simon "we haven't eaten for quite a time and we're really quite hungry. What restaurants do you recommend?"

"We don't have many public restaurants as most Muscovites eat at home. The few we still have are very busy and the food is not so good. But a new private restaurant opened recently. It is western style which means it's very expensive. It's called Optimist and it's just round the corner. I can call them and reserve a table for you, if you like."

Simon looked at Amira who nodded and he said "that would be great. A table at the earliest possible time, please." After calling the restaurant, Nina told them a table for two was available immediately.

They arrived at the Optimist and were shown to their table. The bar was full of customers drinking liquor and talking loudly but hardly anybody was eating there. The owner came up and proudly explained that the restaurant was brand new; he had received a license from the Government two weeks ago to open the first privately-owned restaurant in Moscow. He explained the menu and then said regrettably that only the fish was available. And he literally meant that only the fish was available because nothing else came with it – no bread, no vegetables, no rice and no salad.

Once they had both greedily eaten their plates of boiled fish (name unknown), their waiter came over and asked if they would like some hot tea and vodka. They both politely declined but Simon asked for some more fish for both of them. The waiter looked very surprised replying "you had the last two pieces. We'll have some more tomorrow, we hope. You can come back then." They both smiled at each other and paid their bill.

"Thank goodness we brought some chocolate with us. We need to find some other food source otherwise we are going to starve" Simon complained. "Welcome to Russia" smiled Amira. "Now let me explain about the old lady outside our room."

She continued "She is known as a babushka which is Russian for grandma. Don't let that name fool you. They are employed in hotels throughout Russia and Eastern Europe to keep an eye on rooms occupied by foreigners. They report back to the hotel manager who is a Party member and who in turn sends a report to the local police who may contact the KGB if they find anything suspicious."

"But why check on us. What information do we have?"

"We are foreigners. You are American and I'm Hungarian. They are just carrying out orders."

"Are we in danger?"

"No, so long as we are careful. Remember what I told you before we left France."

They returned to the hotel and spent an uneventful night in their room making sure that they did not discuss anything controversial.

The following morning they came down for breakfast around 8a. There was a long line of hotel guests in the canteen waiting patiently for food. Simon asked what the problem was and a fellow-American told him that the hotel hadn't yet received its food allowance for breakfast. "You could go and try to find somewhere else to eat but hotels get their food before other places so I'm going to wait."

After 90 minutes the staff announced breakfast would be served – stale white bread, sliced rounds of something that looked like meat and watery orange juice.

"We have to find some food. We've finished our chocolate that we brought."

Amira agreed and said "leave it to me. After we have finished here I will go and see the manager."

"What can he do?"

"There's always a way to get round a problem. Let me have some more of your dollar bills."

"Are you going to bribe him? You mustn't, you'll get arrested."

"Stay here. I've done this before. I'll see you back in our room."

Simon walked past the babushka and tried to make conversation with her. No luck. She pretended she was deaf pointing to her ears and shrugging her shoulders. "A deaf spy! You have to be kidding!" he muttered.

Amira came back after 30 minutes with enough passes to get at least one good meal each a day at Cafe Radoff. "This is an old restaurant that is always busy. We can't reserve a table but these passes will get us in. The food is traditional Russian. You will like it."

"Right now I'd like any food. Good job, Amira. How much did that cost?"

"Nothing. The manager's mother is originally from Budapest and he speaks Hungarian quite well. I guess he took pity on me and gave me these passes free of charge."

They immediately left for the restaurant and they found the food at Café Radoff was plentiful and buffet-style with a fixed price; the passes allowed them to eat there only once a day so they took full advantage of their hotel manager's kindness and made sure they left the Café with full stomachs.

The following day they went sightseeing. They returned to the tank traps and read the inscriptions memorializing the sacrifices that the Soviet military and the Moscow citizenry had made. The Russians had fielded more than a million soldiers and a thousand highly-maneuverable and well-armored tanks, placed into multiple defensive lines which had been dug by the hands of Moscow women and children. They halted the bloodshed the Nazis had been creating in their country.

After visiting the memorial, Simon and Amira made their way to the Kremlin and Red Square experiencing for the first time the Moscow subway system. What struck Simon was that it was so clean and inexpensive. There were no panhandlers and no adverts just beautiful pieces of art everywhere. It felt more like an art gallery rather than a transport system.

An elderly British couple kindly took their photo outside the Kremlin Wall. They hurriedly said their goodbyes to the Brits saying they had tickets for the Bolshoi Ballet that evening. On the way to the Theater, they decided to stop at the hotel. There was a message waiting for them at reception. The note said "Guests will not be allowed to access their rooms on the 6th, 7th and 8th floors from tomorrow night at 6p until 10a the following morning as we are hosting a high level delegation from our fraternal comrades in the Cuban Government. If needed, accommodation and breakfast will be provided for one night at the Workers' Gymnasium on Molotov Street. You must take all your luggage with you. Transport will be provided leaving at 4p tomorrow and returning at 12noon on the following day. Anyone who does not comply with this request will be arrested by the security police."

"We'll cope with this tomorrow. Right now I'm looking forward to seeing The Nutcracker. Let's leave now and make sure we can get seated." Amira agreed.

The next day after their usual mundane breakfast they asked Nina at the front desk what the rooms would be like at the Workers' Gymnasium. She told them not to worry and that they would be safe and it was for only a few hours. "20 hours actually" complained Simon. It turned out that the one night at the Workers' Gymnasium was an experience which neither of them wanted to repeat. The place was hot and smelly; only lumpy cots were available to sleep on; there were no dividers separating men from women; washing facilities were minimal. They had to compete for resources with the visitors who came to work out during all hours of the day and night. Breakfast consisted of stale rye bread, borscht (vegetable) soup and hot tea. At 12 noon the transport arrived to take them back to their hotel where they enjoyed hot showers and a change of clothes. Afterwards, they made their way to Café Radoff for a substantial meal.

Over next the few days they did some final sightseeing before returning to Chamonix. They had a relaxing return journey on Air France. They discussed how they felt about what they had seen and heard during their short stay. Simon expressed his views with a surprising depth of feeling – "I found our whole visit eye-opening. We did history at school – the Greeks, the Romans, American history from the Revolution to present day. We touched on the two World Wars and the Holocaust, discussed the Korean War and the Vietnam War. I have learned so much more these past few days as if I have done a crash course in European History."

"What conclusions have you drawn?" Amira asked.

"The biggest impression that I shall take with me is the sadness and despair we saw in all the Russians we met. They seemed bewildered. They have no faith in Gorbachev's attempts to reform Communism. Their system of government is slowly breaking down. Supplies of food are unreliable and everyday things we take for granted in the West don't work. You told me that the population is declining and that alcoholism and corruption are the only growth industries. There's one abiding conclusion that I will have forever. It doesn't matter where tyranny comes from – either the Left or the Right – it is still tyranny. Tyranny leads to persecution, corruption and inevitably to slaughter. You can dress it up so it looks attractive and beguiling with fancy parades, colorful uniforms, imposing titles but it is still tyranny. This visit has helped me make up my mind what sort of career I want to pursue when I return home. I'm nineteen and I'm going to go to college to study modern languages and then join the UN or the Foreign Service or a charity where hopefully I can help spread the word about our system of government – of freedom to choose what you want to read, where you want to live, whom you want in power and so on. Tell me what you have learned Amira?"

"Nothing new really. The visit reinforced my views about Russia and Communism. When are planning to go back to the USA?"

"I don't know yet, Amira. I want to go the Berlin Wall first, though.

Right now I'm so tired. I need a nap."

With that Simon yawned and fell asleep and Amira wondered what Simon decision to return to the States meant for her. She was falling in love with this young American but she knew it was not being reciprocated. She might have to cool their relationship once they returned to Chamonix. She noted Simon had not suggested she went to Berlin with him.

8 ONE UNHAPPY AMBASSADOR 2020

Guy was very pleased with Simon's excellent progress at the clinic.

"You are amazing Simon. You are using your new hand as if you've had it since birth. I congratulate you on your perseverance."

"Thank you, Guy, for all your help. Does that mean I can return home and to the Embassy sooner that you indicated?"

"Today is Wednesday. I think we can discharge you first thing Friday but you must rest at home until Monday. Don't forget to continue with your daily exercises. We don't want the hand to seize up. How does that sound?"

"Good. Suzanne and Phillipe are visiting me today for lunch. I'll ask Béatrice to pick me up on Friday."

As Guy left the room, Simon switched on the TV to catch the news. The incriminating video of the Russian President had been released that morning. The "talking heads" were expounding on the implications of the story – was it fake? What would the White House say? What would happen to American/ Russian relations? And so on and so forth. Simon sat back and waited for Dirty Harry's explosive call.

It came within a few minutes like a hurricane.

"I suppose all this is your doing. You are making me look like a fool and making our foreign policy look completely f***ed up. You'll pay for this, Simon. I promise you."

"You're referring to the video of the Russian President fornicating with two young men, Ambassador?"

"Of course I damn well am! And there's no need to be so explicit!"

"My network obtained the video some months ago following the CIA's decision at the highest level to undermine and shame the Russian President and send **'a don't f*** with our democracy message'** to his cabinet. The video is not a fake. The President is gay or maybe bisexual or whatever but he is for sure a raging hypocrite. It's time the Russian people know the truth about him."

"I specifically told you to roll up your network and start infiltrating Sunni Moslem groups in Europe. Where's the plan? And don't tell me you are still recuperating!"

"I do remember what you asked me to do." Simon had to stall Dirty Harry's ranting and decided to include some of his high-grade diplomatic bullshit (that is, lies) in his argument with the Ambassador.

Simon went on "Firstly your directive about my network is unconstitutional. Secondly, you know very well that I report to the Head of Station in Paris on these matters, not the Ambassador or anyone else in Department of State. Anyway, the President-Elect is not permitted to make such decisions until after his inauguration. Nor is the current President as he's being impeached and most of his cabinet is facing prosecution. Washington is a complete mess incapable of making rational decisions. Ask the CIA Director and see what he says about the video. You need to know that it took me 12 years to build the intelligence network you've asked me to destroy. These are good people who are allies and who have been working to support democratic governments and movements in their home countries. My current network is not structured to infiltrate Moslem groups. If I get such a directive from the CIA, it will take time, maybe years. It might be better to get that intelligence from other existing sources."

"How"

"I'm not discussing this any more on an insecure phone line. I will run it by you next week."

The Ambassador was silent. Simon sounded as if he knew what he was talking about. He would have to check it out for himself. However, he would remember this episode and make sure that Simon paid for his insolence and disobedience sometime in the future.

"Well, Simon, I'll look forward to that. For your information the President-Elect is planning to lift sanctions on Russia, let Russia takeover Ukraine completely and invite Russia to join the Five Eyes organization to share all our and our Allies' high-level intelligence."

(Five Eyes, often abbreviated as **FVEY**, is an intelligence alliance comprising Australia, Canada, New Zealand, the UK and the USA. These countries, with a similar common law legal inheritance, are parties to the multilateral treaty for joint cooperation in signals intelligence. The Five Eyes relationship is one of the most comprehensive and overt espionage alliances in history.)

This gets worse, Simon said to himself. He said goodbye to Dirty Harry. Almost immediately his new hand began to throb – the sensation wasn't painful but the blood was pulsating and it felt as if it was trying to explode out of his new hand and forearm. This worried Simon and he wondered if he should contact Guy. But then he would probably recommend that Simon remain at the clinic into the following week. "I'm sure it'll pass" he assured himself.

The highlight of this day was going to be the visit of his two children, Suzanne and Phillipe. While he waited for them he recalled the complexity of the plan to get this video made.

Some years back he was participating in a cultural event promoting American Art at the US Embassy in Istanbul, Turkey. (His colleagues at the Embassy had invited him as he was the leading expert in Europe on running such cultural exchanges.) On the second day of the program he was approached by a well-dressed, polite Turkish gentleman who introduced himself as an admirer of American Art. They exchanged cards and Simon noticed that Mehmet's title was printed in English as Commissioner of the Turkish Revenue Administration. Mehmet explained that he had visited the US many times both on business and vacation; he had great admiration for the American way of life and great respect for their democratic institutions.

"With the collapse of the Soviet Empire there are many former Soviet countries in the Caucasus who want to be friends with the USA. Turkey still has significant commercial ties with these countries dating back to the Ottoman Empire. Our Government is now reviving those old relationships with these predominantly Moslem countries. If the US is looking to expand its influence peacefully in the Moslem world, then I can be of service to you and your country. You must know that they hate the Russians. And they have little interest in the Chinese."

Simon thanked Mehmet for his offer of help and asked him what sort of recompense he would be looking for. Mehmet smiled saying "US$ of course. We can negotiate the terms later, Simon."

Another example of Walter's advice – greed, reflected Simon.

Simon said he would like to meet with him again privately before he returned to Paris. He agreed to call Mehmet in a few days once the cultural program had finished. Later that day he approached the US Ambassador at the Embassy in Istanbul to ask what he knew about Mehmet. "Nothing at all. I suggest you contact Head of Station here. We don't have any spies in this Embassy" he said with an air of superiority.

On an embassy encrypted line Simon checked with Walter Talbot back in Paris.

"What do you know about the Head of Station in Istanbul" he enquired.

Walter replied "he's OK. But why do you want to know?" Simon explained his conversation with Mehmet and wanted to make sure that the guy was on the up and up.

"Let me check Mehmet out and I'll get back to you in a couple of hours. If you run him by my colleague in Istanbul he might prefer to keep him as a contact for himself. That's if Mehmet is any good."

True to his word Walter got back to Simon. He reported that Mehmet was 'clean', was happily married, was a devout Moslem, was in good standing with the Government and had no debts. With that confirmation Simon met again with Mehmet at a coffee-house close to the Bosphorus. From then on Mehmet gave information to Simon which he relayed to Washington and at times to Walter about developments in the Caucasus that might help US political and commercial activities. The information was helpful but fairly low-grade, however Simon agreed to pay Mehmet in the hope that something more promising would turn.

One day he reached out to Simon, who was in Paris, saying "I'm flying to Paris tonight and I must see you urgently tomorrow. I'm staying at the Georges Cinq. Can you meet me for breakfast at 8a? This is important, Simon." Simon readily agreed.

After they had small-talked their way thru an excellent breakfast of café au lait, croque monsieur and croissants, they walked along the Rue Pierre Charron and Mehmet explained his reason for the urgent meeting.

"One of my contacts, a Somali woman living in the Caucasus region, has let me know about a group of young Moslem democratic activists in Chechnya who want to damage the reputation of the Russian President. The Somali woman's husband and his family were liquidated by Russian Special Forces. She wants to revenge their deaths.

"The Chechen activists accused the Russian President of ordering the murder of their relatives during the various Russian invasions of their region. Somehow they found out that the Russian President is gay or bi-sexual although he has fervently passed anti-gay laws. They want to publish proof of his hypocrisy as revenge. They are going to travel to Tirana, Albania in a few days to get financial support for their cause. I think you should meet them."

Simon was somewhat cautious about his response. "What are they planning to do, Mehmet?"

"I do not know the details. What I do know is they are distantly-related to members of the Russian-backed Chechnya government and somehow they got to know of some young Russian gays who regularly meet the President at his dacha outside St. Petersburg. The President invites other like-minded members of his circle (Cabinet Ministers, oligarchs, etc.) to these parties where there's plenty of alcohol and sex orgies. This group of activists need financing to purchase some hi-tech surveillance equipment and record what the President and his friends get up to. Also they need the means to publish the material."

"What are the names of these activists, Mehmet?"

"They have code names only. Argun and Shali. Names of two cities in

Chechnya."

Simon agreed to travel to Tirana so long as Mehmet came with him. Simon used a false German passport with the name of Erich Schneider, Agricultural Consultant. He obtained some literature and specifications on the latest Wi-Fi enabled driverless tractors, harvesters and planters and made sure he could maintain a reasonable discussion on this equipment in both German and Russian in case he was asked any questions upon arriving. Also he had some business cards printed and took a list of leading Albanian agriculturists that he planned to talk to.

 They both arrived in Tirana on the same flight and stayed at the same hotel where Mehmet introduced his contact, the Somali woman, plus Argun and Shali. Simon introduced himself using his fake name but did not share his real or fake career. He knew there was considerable monitoring of people and conversations by the Albanian security services and the same could be said for the Russians and the Americans who were both active in this part of the Balkans. So they walked to a large park near the hotel and discussed with Argun and Shali their plans to humiliate the Russian President.

He was impressed with the detail of their plan. He explained that he couldn't authorize the transfer of funds for their cause but they would hear back via Mehmet in a few days. He would recommend that an initial payment of US$50,000 be made followed by a final payment of the same amount once the video had been received and confirmed as authentic and not a fake. Argun and Shali were very happy with the offer and accepted it immediately. Mehmet received an initial payment of $15K for his introduction to Argun and Shali with the promise of another $25K should the video project be authentic.

As Simon and Mehmet walked back to the hotel, Simon said he needed to set up some visits over the next few days to agricultural experts in Tirana to maintain his cover. Fortunately, the experts who agreed to meet him at both the University and several big corporations were very impressed by a visit from a leading German consultant and were delighted to spend a few hours of their time drinking Raki and sharing their country's vision for improving Albania's agricultural economy.

Mehmet agreed to fly directly back to Istanbul. Simon decided to return to Paris by way of Sofia, Bulgaria. As he was going thru Customs at Tirana Airport he was taken aside by a plain-clothes official from SHISH – the American- backed Albanian internal security service. He politely quizzed Simon (Erich) about his visit, where did he go and whom did he meet. It was obvious to Simon that he already knew the answers to all his questions. Fortunately, he seemed satisfied and wished Simon safe travels on his way to Sofia.

Simon wanted to meet another contact of his in Sofia. His name was Antonin. He was a former high-ranking member of the Bulgarian Committee for State Security (DS) under Soviet rule. Following the collapse of the Soviet Empire, Antonin started his own private security service providing equipment and services to the Bulgarian Central Bank, leading commercial banks and large retailers throughout Bulgaria. He was not a pleasant man to be with. He had unsmiling eyes, small stature, a limp handshake and worst of all he had chronic bad breath. Whenever he spoke to someone, he was always in very close proximity almost intimidatingly so and spoke softly as if he were sharing top secret information. In those situations one always received the full 'benefit' of his halitosis.

His one redeeming feature was his passionate love for art and music. He loved to attend exhibitions, festivals and concerts throughout Europe. Sometime ago at the Opéra de Paris on one occasion when Béatrice was part of the orchestra playing Béla Bartók's musical score for Bluebeard's Castle, Walter introduced Simon to Antonin during the intermission. Although Simon was more interested in watching the opera, he was impressed with Antonin's willingness to provide information that could help his work.

(Before Antonin returned to Sofia, they met up later that week at a more secluded location where they could talk freely. He explained to Simon that he was not looking for any financial gain – he just wanted to help the USA. He ran a good business, Bulgaria was now stable and a strong supporter of NATO. Despite their many cultural and religious ties with Russia, he preferred to keep the Russian Bear at arm's length and saw America as the best way to prevent aggression from the East. Simon thought – a pragmatic mixture of fear and idealism!)

Without sharing too much information, Simon wanted to get Antonin's thoughts about his discussions in Tirana. Antonin confirmed the rumors about the Russian President's sexual proclivities but "at the end of the day", he said to Simon, "the Russian people won't care. There is too much instability, too much unemployment, too much drunkenness – they have lost their Empire and the respect of the world. They want a leader who is going to fix all this and make Russia powerful and stable again. So what if he likes to have fun with young men?"

"So you think it's not a good idea to release a video showing his hypocrisy."

"I didn't say that. But you must be realistic about the reaction. He will say it's a fake, he will accuse the US of undermining his legitimacy and I expect most Russians will still show their support for him. It might chip away at his invincibility a bit, though."

The phone in Simon's room at the clinic rang and brought him back to the present day. Reception told him he had two visitors waiting for him. He made his way downstairs to meet Suzanne and Phillipe.

As he walked down the stairs to the lobby, Simon remembered that next week would be the twenty-fourth anniversary of his first meeting with Béatrice in 1996. He was stationed in London working with the Cultural Attaché at the US Embassy. Since he spoke Russian and French fluently, he was asked to spend a few days in Paris as the

Moscow Philharmonic Orchestra and the Orchestre de Paris were playing together at the Salle Pleyel – a rare cultural event. He was introduced to members of both orchestras including the conductors and event managers and spoke with staff from the Russian Embassy and the French Ministry of Culture. Everyone was very impressed with the young American's ability with language and his knowledge of European music (he had done a lot of homework on this topic before he left the UK). He had one particularly interesting conversation with a member of the Russian delegation – a conversation which would lead to a very useful relationship later in his diplomatic career.

Both orchestras played exceptionally well. At the end the whole audience stood up, clapped loudly and shouted "encore, encore" for a full 10 minutes. Simon had an excellent view of the musicians as he was seated in the front row. One of the violinists caught his eye; she was slim, dark-haired and had the most beautiful smile he had ever seen. Eventually after playing a few extra scores, both orchestras left through an exit door and made their way down to a reception area where light refreshments and beverages had been arranged for all the musicians and select members of the audience.

Simon and his colleagues had been invited to mingle and chat with the musicians. There were over 60 folks in the reception area and they kept coming. He had lost sight of the violinist who had caught his eye. He decided to keep away from the crowd and quickly scan the reception area checking to see where she was. "Oh, there she is" he said to himself excitedly. She was in a small group talking, eating and drinking. He wandered over and asked her with a smile "pardonnez-moi mademoiselle but what do you recommend to eat and drink here?"

She turned her head and replied "what makes you think I am not married, monsieur?"

Simon was impressed by this very direct woman and glancing into her face he noticed that she had the most beautiful silver-grey eyes luminesced with flashes of green light. He was captivated. "Excuse me if I've made a mistake but you're not wearing a ring. But allow me to introduce myself. My name is Simon Montfort and I'm with the US Embassy. I just wanted to compliment you on that extraordinary performance tonight. I thoroughly enjoyed it. So what do you recommend?" (While Simon was trying to make sure that she was not married before he flirted with her, he was struck by the shape and condition of her hands. They looked strong and capable but they were so smooth and unblemished like pale alabaster. The hands of a true artist who could make a violin sing!)

 "Well Simon, it's nice to meet you and my name is Béatrice Dubois de Prisque. All the food is excellent but I recommend the Pinot Noir as the best beverage. What do you do at the Embassy when you aren't attending concerts?"

"Currently I work for the Cultural Attaché at the Embassy in London. I was asked to attend this concert to help out with translation."

"Your French is excellent. What other languages do you speak?"

"German, Russian and Spanish. Let's move to a quieter room. It's so noisy here with all these people."

"Of course. I'd like that."

So Simon and Béatrice spent the next two hours talking about their careers, their hopes and their families. Béatrice told him that she had been playing with the Orchestre de Paris for three years after graduating from the Conservatoire de Paris in 1993. Time flew by too quickly and they both had to leave as the various groups were getting ready to go. They exchanged phone numbers and addresses and promised each other to keep in touch and visit. Simon said he really wanted to get a diplomatic posting to the US Embassy in Paris but it might be some years away. He promised he would return soon if not on business then for pleasure. They said their goodbyes kissing each other on both cheeks in the Parisian way. Waving their au revoirs, they looked forward to seeing each other again very soon.

As Simon descended the stairs at the clinic he noticed Suzanne and Phillipe sipping pastis in the bar area. (A bar in a clinic might seem an anomaly but not in France where wine and liquor are all part of the 'joie de vivre' of French life.)

Both embraced their father calling him "papa" and expressing their delight as he demonstrated how well his new hand and forearm were working. Suzanne was Simon's favorite as she reminded him so much of his wife. She worked as a fashion designer with Balmain (one of the leading couturiers in Paris) having attended ESMOD Paris where she studied under some of the finest designers in the world.

Philippe was still a student working on his Master's degree in speech pathology at the UPMC in Paris. He was mildly autistic and had chosen this course of study as he wanted to help fellow-sufferers enjoy more fulfilling lives. Also he was brilliant at Math and could have easily got his Masters or higher in that area.

Suzanne shared with Simon that "Maman is very worried about you, Papa. She says you ought to take off more time from work to make sure you have fully recovered from your operation. She also mentioned that you seemed very preoccupied and secretive. What is going on?"

Typical Suzanne, straight to the point like me thought Simon.

"I'm just having a tough time at the Embassy, that's all. Nothing to worry about. The new Ambassador is a boor. Doesn't have much idea about diplomacy, in particular cultural affairs. He has come up with some really weird ideas that go right against what I believe in. These things happen. It's politics! So tell me about the fashion world."

"Well, I'm off to Milan soon where I'll be showing some of my designs during their Fashion Week. I shall probably take some vacation time while I'm in Italy and visit Maman while she's playing in Rome and then go to Florence for a few days."

"Taking vacation already! You haven't been there 5 minutes! Anyway I'm sure the showing will be great success and your mother will love to explore the beauty of Rome with you."

What Simon did not know was that Suzanne was a very successful gambler. Her specialty was blackjack. Whenever she visited foreign cities she made sure she visited the best casinos and gambled there until the early hours. She was highly disciplined. Once she had made a return of 200% or lost 25%, she would quit. She met a lot of wealthy and influential people at these casinos, from all walks of life; some were a bit dubious but some of them could potentially help her career in the fashion world.

Philippe was quiet and self-contained. He loved his parents and sister but their life styles and careers were alien to him. His joy in life was not excitement or wealth or wonderful art but just simply the pleasure he derived from helping an autistic person begin to communicate better with the outside world through the power of improved speech. As well as studying for his Masters, Philippe worked at S.P.R.I.N.T in Paris as a speech pathologist (S.P.R.I.N.T was founded in Paris in 1986 as a non-profit organization to work with children of all ages with special needs).

Simon turned to his son and asked about his studies. "Going well, thank you" he replied "but I want to know what is going to happen about Maman's hearing. Does she need to learn sign language while she can still hear? I can learn to sign at S.P.R.I.N.T and then I can teach her. What do you think, Papa?"

"I think you are a very caring son, Philippe. Maman would be very proud of you if she could hear you speak like this. Don't you agree, Suzanne?"

"Of course" she replied.

"But Maman will be changing her career after her performance in Rome. That will be her last public event. She will focus on composing and arranging music. That will be much better for her ears. I'm not dismissing your kind suggestion but I hope her hearing will stabilize so she won't need to learn to sign. Let's wait until she gets the results of her next hearing test."

Simon suggested they go and have lunch at a local restaurant which specialized in rustic cuisine and continue to talk about family stuff while enjoying an excellent lunch and some fine Burgundy.

9 BERLIN WALL NOVEMBER 1989

I n November 1989 a series of peaceful protest movements in nearby Eastern Bloc countries—Poland and Hungary in particular—caused a chain reaction in East Germany that ultimately resulted in the demise of the Berlin Wall. After several weeks of civil unrest, the Communist East German government announced on 9 November 1989 that all East German citizens could visit West Germany and West Berlin. Crowds of East Germans crossed and climbed onto the Wall, joined by West Germans and international civil rights activists on the other side in a celebratory atmosphere of **Bringing down that Wall.**

Simon, Walter and John had arrived in West Berlin on November 6th. They had rented a pick-up and bought as much 'wall-destroying 'equipment as they could carry. They booked themselves into a low-cost student hostel near AlexanderPlatz in the British Sector. (The military authorities in both the American and French-controlled sectors would not permit them and their equipment to approach the Wall). AlexanderPlatz was still recovering from the massive demonstration comprising of more than 500,000 protesters of November 4th demanding freedom of speech, free elections and the destruction of the Wall.

Their plan was to drive to the Wall the following morning November 7th after a decent meal and a goodnight's sleep so they were ready for a full day of 'wall demolition'. Over dinner at a restaurant near the hostel, they chatted about their individual plans for returning to their home countries. Walter had already decided to follow his parents' footsteps and join the CIA. His father had been an Operations Officer in the CIA Clandestine Unit and his mother had been a Communications Officer in their Enterprise & Support Unit. "Once I get back home in the New Year I'll be mailing my application."

John French said that he came from a military background. Right now his elder brother was in Northern Ireland working as part of a counter-terrorism unit. Obviously he did not say much about what he did but John said his brother spent a lot of his time outside lying in cold, wet ditches waiting for the bad guys. John was thinking of joining the Customs and Excise Drug Interdiction team. Simon wasn't interested in spying or surveillance and told his friends his preference was to become a Foreign Service Officer with the Department of State. "You know, become a diplomat. One of my uncles was a diplomat serving in a number of countries after WW2; he would be more than willing to advise me and introduce me to other former diplomats so I could make sure this is the career for me."

The following day they all set off early for the Wall not quite sure what they would see and what would happen. They soon spotted the 12ft. high concrete blocks that snaked their evil way for 27 miles dividing West Berlin from East Berlin. A second wall had been built some 110 yards further into East German territory to provide a 'killing ground' so the Vopos (People's Military Police) could easily spot and slaughter escaping refugees. The original houses contained between the two Walls had been razed. The 110 yard 'killing ground' had been covered with raked sand or gravel. Hundreds of watch towers complete with machine guns and searchlights had been installed; rolls of barbed wire and heavy wooden obstacles had been put in place to try and deter escapees. Despite all these precautions over 5,000 East Germans had escaped to the West Berlin during the Wall's 28 years' existence; however, some 200 innocent Germans had been slaughtered in the 'killing ground' some had been left wounded as they bled to death and gasped their last breaths lying on the smooth, raked gravel of East Berlin.

A jeep carrying four armed members of the British Military Police suddenly appeared from nowhere and a Warrant Officer stepped out quickly ordering Simon and his friends to stop their vehicle. "You will have to leave your vehicle here and proceed to the Wall on foot" said the MP in an East London accent. Looking at Walter as he appeared the oldest, he said "You and your mates can join the crowd assembling here if you want but hammering is forbidden as you can see from all the large signs that are around here."

Some of these signs had been painted on the full height of the Wall.

Walter nodded and noticed that a long line of mostly young people were standing quietly some three feet or so from the Wall. Pointing to the line of people stretching in both directions for what appeared to be miles, Walter asked the MP "what are they doing?"

"Waiting for us to bugger off. As soon as we leave they will return to trying to destroy the Wall" he said with a slight smile. "These guys are very orderly and law abiding. They don't want trouble. They know that the next MP patrol will drive past in 2 hours' time so they will hammer away until then."

Jumping back into his vehicle he said with a wink "I hope you put your demolition equipment to good use."

The three of them watched as the MP's vehicle drove away slowly down the line of people. They could see how the line started to change shape as the protesters stopped hammering and stood back from the Wall until the MP's jeep had driven past them. Then they started hammering again. And so this game between the protesters and the MP's continued until their jeep drove out of sight.

Walter and Simon turned to John and said "Brit humor?"

"Certainly was. Well, we have two hours before they return. We'd better get working."

With that they ran back to their vehicle, loaded up with as much of their equipment as they could carry and walked carefully to the Wall. They quickly found a section where just a few people were hammering and got to work. They soon realized that the Wall was made from reinforced concrete with the rebar enmeshed every foot in each four foot wide concrete block. It was going to be hard work without power equipment. Then John shouted "I'm through, I'm through!" He was hitting the Wall like a madman and had a made an oval-shaped hole round a piece of rebar. Eventually, once the hole was wide enough to see through to the other side he stopped wielding his sledgehammer and peered through the gap.

Simon and Walter were standing near him and noticed him slowly move away from the Wall close to tears. "I can see the killing ground. It's so quiet, so desolate, so menacing to look at. I wonder how many Germans were shot here in cold-blood by their own people as they ran to freedom. Take a look."

John was the most sensitive of the three of them and they were not surprised by his reaction. Simon agreed it was a horrible sight – one which he would never forget.

"We're making history, guys. We'll be able to tell our children and our grandchildren about our small contribution" Simon said encouragingly to John.

So they continued hammering away making more and more holes in the Wall and playing the 'game' with the British MP patrols. They took a short lunch of Frankfurters and beer at a stand erected recently by an enterprising West Berliner to provide refreshments for the protesters. Simon got chatting with the other people helping to destroy the Wall. They were mostly young West Berliners both students and workers who taken time off like Simon and his friends. He found out that on the following day some construction workers were bringing in large cranes and cutters to remove complete concrete blocks.

"What will the MP's do?" he asked.

One of the West Berliners said "Who cares? Are they going to arrest all of these people in front of the International Press who have just started arriving in droves? I don't think so. By tomorrow there will be no more British Military patrols. I think the Berlin Police will be here to keep order but they won't stop us. They're on our side."

Simon told the others about the cranes coming. Walter sounded very pleased "using a sledgehammer is damned hard work. I'd rather be on a construction site in Chamonix. So cranes would be great."

They called it a day mid-afternoon and took their equipment back to their pick-up and drove slowly back to their hostel. Their muscles had had a thorough workout and they were looking forward to some hot showers before they went sightseeing and grabbing some dinner later on.

Being near AlexanderPlatz, there were plenty of restaurants, bars, pubs and casinos for tourists to visit. The square was the transport hub for West Berlin so they could travel easily to visit the Reichstag and the Kurfuerstendamm. Unfortunately, the famous Brandenburg Gate had been closed since 1961.

While they ate dinner of schnitzel, potato salad and beer at a local bar, a TV news anchor was excitedly reporting that East German citizens were driving across AlexanderPlatz into West Berlin. Simon translated the German news to his friends and said "We ought to get back to the Wall and see what's happening ourselves." They both agreed and jumped into their pick-up and drove straight for the

Wall. As they approached they saw a line of old, two-stroke Trabant cars driving slowly across the empty 'killing ground' into AlexanderPlatz where unarmed West German Police were checking each vehicle and its occupants. The passengers were all smiling, waving their East German passports and shaking hands with as many people as they could on the West German side of the Wall. (The Trabant was a slow, smelly symbol of the East German regime – many car enthusiasts described the vehicle as 'a spark plug with a roof ').

The cars were crawling their way over the old cobblestones of the dark Platz with their dim headlights illuminating the path a few feet in front of them. Each vehicle was full of East Germans with just a few prized possessions – they didn't know how long they would have to wait before they could return to their homes and bring back more of their belongings.

The three friends ran to the open section of the Wall and took photos of the Trabant procession and joined in the celebration. Simon broke away from the group and tried to walk towards the East German side but was quickly stopped by the police asking to see his German passport. "I just want to see what it looks like over there" he explained.

"We will not permit you to go any further. Even if you were German, we would advise you strongly against going any further. The Stasi are still active and will have no qualms about harming any nosy visitors. Please go back."

"What the hell were you thinking?" shouted Walter. "There's a revolution going on over there. So far it's been peaceful. You want to cause an international incident?"

"Okay, okay, I was just being curious."

They stayed for a few more hours watching more and more Trabants. Simon had to be content with chatting with some of the escapees about their lives in the GDR and how they had been allowed to leave. Everyone he talked to was very discreet and preferred not to say much about living conditions in the East in case word somehow got back and their relatives were punished. But they did explain how they were able to leave. Several high-ranking members of the National People's Army wanted to escape from East Berlin with their families. They knew many East Berliners were desperate to leave and they persuaded a large group to meet at the Berliner Fernsehturm (Berlin TV Tower) with the promise of guaranteed escape. They blended in with this large group of East Berliners and deceived the Vopos using forged departure permits issued by the GDR. Because of the confusion and lack of clear leadership in East Germany they had no problem crossing into West Berlin.

On their way back to the hostel late that night Simon was elated "I can't believe we experienced so much history today. I can't wait to see what happens tomorrow when the cranes come. I've been told that the crowds will be enormous."

Simon was right. There were hundreds of protesters milling round the Western side of AlexanderPlatz waiting patiently for the cranes to arrive. Two mobile cranes were driven into the area around 8a that morning. Each crane came with a team of expert operators who immediately began installing the stabilizers and lifting gear. Small groups of protesters managed to get up onto the top of the concrete blocks to remove the anchors; Simon decided to join one of these groups. What he did not realize was that he was standing on a section of the Wall that had no rebar; so as he removed the anchors the sections gave way and he quickly fell to the ground. Pieces of concrete fell onto him pinning his left hand and arm to the ground. He was in a state of shock and was suffering a lot of pain but he was conscious. John and Walter saw him fall, ran over to him and carefully lifted off the pieces of the Wall that were pinning him down. His left hand and arm were bloody. A military ambulance was on the scene in minutes and whisked him away to the British Military Hospital with his friends following in their pick-up. Lucky for Simon, a preeminent orthopedic surgeon from the UK was visiting the hospital on that same day and he was asked to assist in the OR. His name was Sir Ian Churchill-Davidson and he specialized in hand/arm surgery.

While the hospital team worked on Simon in the OR for several hours, Walter and John were contacting Simon's family in the USA and Amira in Chamonix. His parents were traveling in the US but Walter got thru to his sister Alice who said she would be flying to Berlin that day. John spoke with Amira who said tearfully "please tell him I love him and I'll be on my way immediately to look after him and bring him back to France."

On November 9th. 1989 following several weeks of civil unrest (the day after Simon's accident) the East German authorities declared that all GDR citizens could visit West Germany and West Berlin. Crowds of East Germans crossed and climbed onto the Wall joined by West Germans on the other side in a celebratory atmosphere. History had been made.

Unfortunately Simon and his two friends missed all the excitement of that final day. Simon was transferred from the OR to the critical care ward. When he woke up he had trouble remembering why his left hand and arm were encased in plaster and why he was in a hospital ward. A staff nurse spoke to him explaining what had happened. She said he had sustained a nasty fall from the Berlin Wall and had severely damaged his hand. She reassured him that the surgeon would see him tomorrow and give him his prognosis. He noticed that her name tag showed the name Elizabeth.

Walter and John visited Simon later that day. Elizabeth told them they could spend no more than 15 minutes with him as he needed to rest and recover. John was clearly smitten with Elizabeth and couldn't take his eyes off her. She smiled and left them alone to see Simon.

He cheered up a lot when he saw his friends and in particular when they told him about the free flow of East Germans thru to West Berlin. They let him know that both Alice and Amira were on their way. "Thanks for contacting them but you ought to know that I want to go back home to the US with my sister Alice. I'm not returning to Chamonix. Amira won't be happy, I know. I have decided to go to college and start working on some career options. Hopefully, they will discharge me from here in a few days so I can get going."

10 GOODBYE AMIRA

The next day the surgeon gently explained to Simon most of the bones in his left hand had been broken and all the nerve links destroyed. The one good thing was that blood was still flowing throughout his limb. But it was so badly damaged that the only possible solution would be amputation and replacement with a prosthetic. That operation would have to be carried out in the US. His arm would remain in plaster for his journey back home. He expressed his regrets to Simon and reassured him that prosthetics had come a long way in recent years. Simon was dumbfounded.

Amira was very distraught when she saw Simon lying in bed with his left hand and arm in plaster. "My love, how are you? Does your hand hurt a lot? When will you be discharged so we can get back home? Chamonix has an excellent hospital specializing in broken bones because of all the winter-skiing accidents. We can get a second opinion. There may be some other options they can recommend. When can you travel?"

Simon felt uncomfortable about sharing his plans to return to America with her but he decided that he had to tell her now. He took a deep breath and explained why he wanted to go back home; that he needed to get a college degree as he was planning to join the Foreign Service.

"But you can get a great education in Europe and we can be together. I will continue to work as an interpreter and support you as much as I can. Once you've got your degree you can apply for a diplomatic career from Europe."

"I don't think that would work. Besides, I want to spend time with my family while they are still healthy. We can still keep in touch by mail and phone. I can still visit you in Europe and you can visit me in the USA."

"Simon, I don't want a long-distance relationship with you. I love you and I want you to be here with me. I want to take care of you until you are fully recovered."

"The prognosis for my hand and arm is not good. The surgeon has recommended amputation and a prosthesis. I'm not having that done. I'm going to live with a withered hand until there's some other solution. So, it will be a long time before I'm fully recovered. I don't want to be a burden to you."

It hurt Amira to hear that her declaration of love was not returned by Simon. Being a very practical woman she accepted his decision and left his side by saying "If you love someone like I love you nothing can be a burden. I wish you well from the bottom of my heart."

Although he had promised to keep in touch with her, she knew that the relationship was finished and she would have to move on. She was tough and had experienced worse situations growing up in Communist Hungary. But she would not forget the way he had treated her!

Simon felt sad as she walked away in a flood of tears. Walter walked past her in the corridor and asked her what the matter was. She replied tartly "Simon can tell you if he wants."

"Amira is very upset. I guess you've told her you're going back to the

States."

"That's right. She took it really badly. I didn't know that she had such strong feelings for me."

Walter changed the subject and asked "do you want to hear some good news?"

"Sure do."

Walter continued "John can't be here with us today because he's dating Elizabeth. They've gone for a late lunch and a quick visit to the Wall. He's been following her around the hospital like a love-sick puppy. In fact, one of senior staff members warned him to be more discreet otherwise he might find himself arrested!"

They both had a smile about John. At last he had found a girl-friend who might share his passion for flora and fauna.

Then Simon remarked "Oh I can see my sister Alice striding thru the ward. She's a doctor, you know. And has an irritating no-nonsense manner that you'll soon witness. Here she comes!"

"Well, Simon. What on earth have you done now?" Alice asked him curtly.

"Good to see you too Alice. Let me introduce my very good friend Walter."

"We spoke on the phone already." She answered pointedly ignoring Walter. "When are you going to be discharged?" Simon updated her on his prognosis and his plans once he was back in the US.

"I want to see your surgeon before we go and get a full prognosis before we leave. I'll arrange some accommodation for myself and get some air tickets for us both."

With that Alice kissed him goodbye and strode off.

Walter spoke first "well you're right. She certainly has an irritating style."

"Churchill-Davidson is going to love her! Still her heart is in the right place."

"What sort of doctor is she then?"

"Doctor of Philosophy – in Archaeology. Loves dead objects. Has a problem with the living" joked Simon.

11 SIMON THE DIPLOMAT

Simon returned to the States and asked his parents if he could stay with them until he got accepted into university. His Mom was delighted to have him home and glad that he intended to pursue further education. "Of course you can stay. This is your home" said his Mom. "Your Dad and I don't travel so much anymore as we want to spend more time together – we aren't getting any younger you know! It'll be great to have you around and you can share all your adventures with us."

"Where's Dad by the way?"

"He'll be back later tonight. He's on his farewell tour before he finally retires. He's not been very well recently. But you know him, he refuses to see the doctor."

"What are his symptoms?"

"He gets tired very quickly. I think all this touring around America is taking its toll on his body."

"OK, Mom, we need to talk with him tomorrow. Let him get a good night's sleep first though."

"He was very upset when he heard about your accident. I think he wants you to have a prosthesis."

"Well, we'll have plenty to talk about tomorrow, won't we?"

"I agree with him about the prosthesis. You can't get a good job with a withered hand."

"If I put a hump on my back I could get a job acting as Richard Third" Simon joked.

"Very funny. Be serious, Simon. You might not be able to become a diplomat."

"So you are saying that having a hook like a pirate would make me a more acceptable candidate?"

"There you go again. Making fun out of a serious subject. Hooks by the way are out of fashion. Let's change the subject. Your uncle is coming over tomorrow and you can quiz him about his career in the Foreign Service."

The following day Simon had a serious discussion with his father about prostheses and his dad's health. Simon agreed to consult a specialist about having a prosthesis if his father agreed to get a check-up. (Simon did actually go and see a specialist but his father lied about going to see a doctor about his health and unfortunately died some months later from stage 4 cancer while Simon was at university. At least his father had decided to cut short his farewell tour after speaking with Simon but had deceived his family into believing his health was fine. This proved to be the final deception from the Master Illusionist. Unfortunately, for Simon's mother there were little savings, no pension and no life insurance payout so she had to return to the stage to pay her bills. Alice was poorly paid as an archaeologist and Simon was an indigent student but he promised to take care of his Mom once he had started his career.)

That same day Simon had a long chat with his uncle who had been an officer in the Visa section of the US Embassy in London for 5 years. He left, returned to the US and started his own international business. He still had some good contacts who had remained in the service far longer than he and promised to set up a few informal meetings for Simon to help him decide the best course for his career.

During the next 4 years Simon studied hard, got a part-time job so he could support his Mom a bit, had some interesting meetings with former diplomats and kept in touch with Amira from time to time. In 1994 he graduated cum laude in Modern Languages covering French, German, Spanish and Russian with a minor in Arabic.

He was fluent in all five languages. With strong backing from his uncle's contacts he applied to the Foreign Service for a career as an FSO. He passed the entrance exam and all the interviews with ease and arrived in the UK to take up his first tour of duty at the US Embassy in Grosvenor Square, London. By then he and Amira no longer kept in touch but he often visited John French and his wife Elizabeth.

Simon threw himself energetically into his work impressing the senior staff with his organizational and linguistic skills; he was often to be seen at high-level meetings acting as an interpreter involving important overseas visitors and was often asked by senior FSO's to manage important activities from start to finish. In 1997 he was promoted to Cultural Attaché and was transferred to the Embassy in Paris.

He and Béatrice were married in 1997 and after their honeymoon in Corsica they returned to Paris and rented a small apartment conveniently located for both of their careers. His work at the Paris Embassy was rather mundane until he got a call from his old friend Walter now CIA Head of Station in Paris. They and their spouses had invited one another over for dinner on several occasions and the four had developed a good friendship although both Simon and Béatrice considered Walter's spouse Mary difficult to get to know. But it was clear that Walter loved her very much.

Walter made it clear that this meeting would involve just the two of them and he characterized it as "business". So they met for dinner in a quiet restaurant where Walter knew he could have a confidential and uninterrupted conversation with Simon. After the usual pleasantries Walter broached the subject carefully.

"How are you finding the work at the Embassy, Simon?"

"It's OK. The Ambassador in the UK gave me more leeway in my work and I got involved in some interesting discussions and activities not directly related to cultural affairs. The Ambassador here is more old school. He wants me to focus only on cultural stuff – you know speeches, presentations, shows and such like. I've told him I'd like to get more involved in other activities but he keeps telling me to be patient. So, what have you got? Something interesting. I hope."

"Ok, so I've been Head of Station for 4 months. I've had to clear out a lot of dead wood as soon as I arrived here. Too much complacency about Russia under Yeltsin. Not enough good, hard intel coming in. I kept being told that Russia was no longer a threat -Yeltsin is a friend to the West, he and Clinton are best buddies, the nuclear threat is dead and so on. I didn't believe it Simon. Yeltsin is weak, doesn't really know what's going on and he's definitely not well. He's a raging alcoholic. The KGB may have changed their initials to FSB but the same thugs run the show. Yeltsin won't last much longer. We must prepare for a tougher, less friendly leader to take over. Corruption is rampant, their economy is tanking. Something is going to happen."

Walter continued in the same vein "I need intel, I need a good network of agents in Eastern Europe in place before the change in power happens. In short, I need your help. You'd be excellent. You have the language skills, your cultural responsibilities allow you to travel easily and meet the right targets. You'd be off the books, you'd set up a covert network, you'd report directly to me. The Ambassador is on board, he shares the same concerns as I do. What do you think?"

One could have knocked Simon over with a feather, he was overwhelmed. "Well. I'm speechless. I wasn't expecting this. It sounds exciting. What types of targets would I be looking for? What sort of information would you need?"

"Good questions. We'll go into that in more detail soon. But basically you'd be looking for targets who are sympathetic to the West and are worried about the Russian Bear. Folks who are well placed in government or commerce who suffered under the Communists. You'd have to be very careful how you approach them but we will teach you. They in turn will have to set up their own network of operatives. Operatives, as well as agents for that matter, typically fall into three groups – the idealists, the money hungry and the afraid. It's amazing how easily citizens will betray their own countries for a fistful of dollars. They are easy to find but can quickly betray their paymasters and turn renegade. The most reliable assets are the afraid. They have something to hide: they could be gamblers, sexual deviants, druggies or have some other vice that is illegal or immoral or both. They will take a lot of work to find. Your agents will have to blackmail their operatives with the promise that their hidden pleasures will remain secret and that any useful intel will be well rewarded. One last tip – keep away from the idealists, they are high maintenance, always questioning everything, too analytical."

"In this way you'll be so well removed from actual field work that you will remain anonymous. Unlike some other spy agencies, we keep our own personnel remote from field operations – your agents will recruit the operatives."

Simon looked thoughtfully at Walter and asked "will this be officially sanctioned by the Head of the CIA or since I will be off the books to use your phrase will the network be subject to 'plausible deniability' leaving me out in the cold as some sort of renegade diplomat?"

"No worries. Off the books means any payments made thru you or directly to your agents or operatives or assets are covert. Payments go through shell companies and discreet Swiss banks."

"How much can I share with Béatrice?"

"Nothing. This is a covert operation. But you may want to find out if any of her contacts in her world of international music could be useful to you."

Over the intervening years Simon had created a master network of intelligence agents in selected European countries – Austria, Bulgaria, Hungary, Turkey and even Russia itself. His cover was never blown as only the Ambassador and Walter knew what he was doing. He hired and trained an excellent support team in the Embassy to execute most of the cultural activities in Paris. He persuaded other US Embassies in European capitals to use his expertise in languages, diplomacy and culture so he could widen his field of operations making sure he did not arouse the embassy staff's suspicions; there would have been severe consequences for Simon, his team and his superiors if his real intentions had been discovered.

The Ambassador agreed with Walter that Beatrice's career and travels gave Simon a unique opportunity to meet an influential group of people who might be willing to work clandestinely for the US Government. Simon was encouraged to accompany Béatrice as she toured foreign capitals. He kept his real intentions well-hidden from her. She thought that he was simply supporting her career.

It took a lot of Simon's time to select the right people and he made some errors of judgement – some big, some small. But he always tried to remember Walter's advice to look for signs of 'fear or greed or even idealism' when conversing with foreign nationals. He would wait for them to make the first approach. At times Walter was amazed by some of Simon's unique masterstrokes. One of these feats is worth telling. It concerned his agent for Russia. His name is Alexei.

He first met Alexei in Paris in 1996 when he was a member of a Russian delegation accompanying the Moscow Philharmonic. (This meeting took place at the same time that Simon met his future, Béatrice, at the Salle Pleyel.) At that time Simon wasn't sure what Alexei's role was. He clearly was not a musician nor a lover of the Arts. Simon suspected he was a sort of 'minder'. Anyway they enjoyed each other's company and promised to keep in touch. Well, as often happens, they didn't contact each other at all. As much as Simon wanted an agent in Moscow, he preferred to play a waiting game and see if Alexei reached out to him.

Some years later, when he was better established in the Paris Embassy, Simon's patience was rewarded with a surprise call from Alexei. He asked "do you remember me Simon?"

Well, of course Simon certainly did, but he played it cool saying "I think we met at the Salle Pleyel, am I right?" To which Alexei responded "you have a good memory. I'm in Paris now and I'd like to meet you in the bookshop of the Galerie National du Jeu de Paume tomorrow say at 9a. I will explain the reason for my meeting when I see you." Without hesitation Simon agreed.

The following day Simon walked to the Jeu de Paume with some trepidation. He had asked Walter to provide some back-up in the bookshop in case the situation got out of hand. He spotted Alexei easily. He appeared to be alone. He was dressed well like a visiting businessman but he looked very worried. They greeted each other and Alexei suggested they went for a walk to the nearby Place de la Concorde. Walter's surveillance team followed them. Alexei told Simon "there's no need for the CIA to follow us. You can call them off. You're safe. I want to ask you a big favor. That's all, Simon."

Simon motioned to the team to stand down but there was one other team member who kept a watchful eye on them as they made their way to the Place de la Concorde.

"How can I help you?" asked Simon.

Alexei slowly wiped a tear from his eyes and explained "It's my daughter. She suffers from Scleroderma. It is a connective tissue disorder and an autoimmune disease which causes changes in the skin, blood vessels, internal organs and muscles. When this disease spreads to the heart, kidney, lungs and GI tract, these organs begin to fail, leading to complications like lung problems, cancer and heart failure. There is no cure available in Russia but recently I heard that a new drug is available in the West. It's proving very successful. I can't get it in Russia. I know it's available in France. Can you help me? I don't know where to go and even if I could find the drug I wouldn't be able to purchase it since I'm not a French citizen. Money is no problem. I'll pay whatever is necessary to get a year's supply. I will take it back home in a diplomatic bag. And I will be in your debt forever, Simon. All you have to do is to ask me – no matter what it is."

Simon couldn't believe his luck! Alexei was showing the classic signs of 'fear' that Walter had mentioned. He expressed his sympathy to Alexei saying that it must be awful for him and his spouse to watch their daughter suffer so much. He was going to reel in Alexei slowly and carefully just like a skilled angler.

"I may be able to help you. My brother-in-law is a doctor. I will ask him about the drug and find out the best way to purchase it. He probably won't want to be involved in the transaction as it would be an ethical maybe a legal issue for him. What's the name of the drug?"

"It's called zexophosate."

"I'll call him later today. How can I reach you?"

"I'm staying at the Georges Cinq and I'm working out of the Russian Embassy over the next few days. I will stay in Paris until I can get the drug."

"What's your role at the Embassy?"

"I lead the Trade Delegation."

Simon was very skeptical about Alexei's title. He was concerned that he might be either Military Foreign Intelligence (GRU) or Federal Security Service (FSB). Simon didn't really care so long as he was not being set up as a blackmail target. He took Alexei's business card and handed over his in exchange. He would check with Walter before he called Guy, his brother-in-law, about the drug. Their meeting ended with Simon promising to get back to Alexei soon.

Walter had given Simon the all clear on Alexei. He assured him that Alexei was not an intelligence officer but a high-ranking bureaucrat in the Russian Central Bank. Nothing untoward was known about him so his request would seem genuine. Walter ended with "Good to Go Simon!" With that assurance Simon contacted Guy and explained the situation. He massaged Alexei's true identity slightly because Guy was very suspicious of anybody from Eastern Europe. "Guy, I have a good friend who is a fellow diplomat and is looking to purchase legally a year's supply of zexophosate to cure his daughter's Scleroderma. He has asked for my help as he cannot get the drug in his own country. I'm not asking you to procure it for him, I would just like to know how he can acquire the drug legally in France."

"No problem. I've read in La Revue de Médecine Interne that the trials have gone really well. He should contact my very good friend Dr. Laurent Biche. He is based at the Tenon Hospital in Paris. If you like I will contact him and give him your friend's name."

"It's probably best to give Dr. Biche my name as my friend does not speak good French."

"As you like. I will let you know what he says."

After various meetings and phone calls Alexei and Simon went to meet Dr. Biche. Fortunately, Alexei brought with him a complete diagnosis of his daughter's condition written in clear English, which Laurent Biche understood as his English was excellent.

"It's clear that you daughter's condition is very serious and the disease has advanced considerably. Typically we would want to get her into our advanced clinical trials that are sponsored by the drug company but she needs immediate treatment. The best I can offer you, Alexei, is that she is treated here at Tenon as a paying patient under the supervision of my team. We would expect her to respond to treatment within a week and improve dramatically at the end of 3 months. All being well she could then return home with a limited supply of the drug which should last for nine months. By then I would hope you could obtain the drug in your country."

Alexei jumped for joy, literally, knocking some memorabilia off Dr. Biche's desk.

"That's wonderful. I am so pleased - so will my wife and daughter! Can you give me some idea of the cost of the 3 month stay?"

"Including all treatment and drugs I would expect the bill to be between $400,000 and $500,000."

"I will have the money wired immediately."

"No need to hurry. Let's wait until your daughter is here. Can she be at my clinic by Monday next week?"

Alexei promised he would apply for her visa and make her travel arrangements immediately. He assured Dr. Biche and Simon that getting his daughter a visa in such a short time frame would be no problem as he had some excellent high-level contacts in the French government. This statement confirmed that Alexei was not a Russian 'spook'.

As they left Laurent Biche's office Alexei could not stop expressing his relief and his excitement. "Firstly, you and I must celebrate tonight with our spouses and enjoy the most excellent meal possible in the whole of Paris. My treat, as you say. I insist. I cannot tell you how much we appreciate your help. Secondly, I must speak with your brother-in-law and thank him personally for introducing me to Dr. Biche."

"Béatrice and I would be delighted to have dinner with you. I can recommend one restaurant in particular – restaurant Benoit on the Rue Saint Martin not far from Notre-Dame We'll see you and your wife there tonight at 7pm. I'll make the reservation. They know me well."

Simon didn't mention calling Guy, hoping that Alexei would soon forget about it.

"Excellent, see you and your lovely wife then."

When you enter the Benoit Paris you immediately feel a comfortable and welcoming atmosphere. The delicate wood paneling, the red velvet banquettes, the intricately-engraved window panes, the large mirrors featuring Beaujolais reproductions and the sound of conversations flowing across the artisan tables – all evoke a sense of epicurean warmth. The Maître d' welcomed Simon and his guests escorting them to their reserved table discretely located in a private lounge.

This dinner would be the first occasion for Béatrice to be meeting a potential agent for her spouse's spy network. She was not aware of Simon's real interest in Alexei as he was following Walter's directive to the letter. Fortunately Alexei's wife, Natasha, was a music lover herself and taught piano in her studio in Moscow so she and Béatrice had a lot in common. They were able to converse in French and English about many different composers and symphony conductors. Alexei was effusive about the help he had received from Simon and Guy, spending a lot of the time over dinner wiping tears of joy from his face. Towards the end of dinner Alexei asked Simon an oblique question about his role at the Embassy. "Simon, you must know that we Russians consider every American diplomat a spy, in particular Cultural Attachés?"

"No, I didn't know that. That's strange because I thought with Yeltsin in power that relations between our two governments were really friendly. Indeed Russia has been invited to attend all NATO meetings as an honorary member. That would have been unheard of a few years ago. So why all the suspicion?"

"I must be careful what I say but Yeltsin is not totally in power, as you say. A new man is being groomed to take over from him soon. Yeltsin has told his cabinet that he wants to appoint a former high-ranking KGB officer as the next President of the Russian Federation. He is a very clever man and very tough. He had a long and successful career in East Germany until the fall of Communism there. He blames the West, in particular your country, for destroying the Soviet Union and for humiliating us now with NATO's expansion close to the borders of Russia. Your government must be careful. But I have said enough, more than enough. This excellent Burgundy has loosened my lips too much."

"What is this guy doing now?"

"He's the mayor of one of our biggest cities. I'm saying no more."

After Simon and Béatrice thanked Alexei and Natasha for their hospitality, they went for a short walk along the nearby Rue de Rivoli. Simon was very pleased with the way he was reeling in Alexei so carefully. His sense of self-satisfaction was interrupted by his wife's question "Is Alexei a spy, Simon?"

"I don't know. His business card says Head of Russian Trade Delegation. When I met him a few years ago I though he was a minder accompanying the Moscow Philharmonic. You just can't tell with the Rooskies." Simon was playing dumb making out he didn't want to talk about it anymore but Béatrice continued.

"What I don't understand is why would he criticize Yeltsin and warn you about his possible successor?"

"I guess he feels very grateful about the treatment plan for his daughter and he wanted to show his appreciation more than just paying for a delightful meal and decided to give me some scuttle-butt on the power struggles in the Kremlin. And as he said, he was well lubricated with Burgundy. Let's enjoy this wonderful evening and not worry about international politics."

"Please don't blow me off, Simon. He was sending you a message; his wife was shocked when he talked about spies and Yeltsin. Didn't you see her face?"

"No, I didn't and I'm not blowing you off. Alexei may be a spy. It's no good speculating. I will ask Head of Security at the Embassy."

"Perhaps you are a spy, Simon" she joked "and he was using his daughter and dinner as cover."

"You've seen too many 007 movies. I can no more be a spy than I can hold you with my left hand."

"Well, give me your right hand and let's enjoy the walk along Rivoli. Then if we cross the Pont Neuf we might be lucky and enjoy the Son et Lumière along the Seine."

So they walked hand-in-hand like a young couple in love enjoying a warm Parisian night joking and smiling about the evening they had just spent. "You got on very well with Natasha didn't you?" Simon mentioned.

"She's a lovely woman but so sad. She's so worried about her daughter. She doesn't know how they can afford the treatment in Paris. It's so expensive. Alexei won't tell her where the money is coming from."

"Hmm, that's interesting. He made out that the cost wouldn't be a problem."

"He must have access to funds that Natasha doesn't know about."

"Could be. You never know with these Rooskies."

Simon mused to himself 'you are too sharp Béatrice, you should be the spy not me". Perhaps Alexei was siphoning off funds from the Central Bank to help pay for his daughter's treatment? If so, that might be another way to get Alexei's cooperation!

They continued walking hand-in-hand enjoying the music coming from speakers along the Seine and Simon said "the sound of those violins has reminded me that you are due to go touring soon. Where are you traveling this time? When do you leave?"

"I'm off to Budapest and Vienna and I'll be leaving next week. We ought to have Charles and his Anna over for dinner before I go. Will you be traveling?"

"I may have to go to Vienna. Perhaps we can meet up. I'll see when Charles is available."

"That's great. If we can meet then I'll introduce you to some very interesting music lovers in Vienna. I know how much you like to meet them. What's taking you to Vienna?"

Simon certainly did like to meet Béatrice's fellow music lovers especially if they were influential and shared his views on Russia. "The Embassy there may need my help on improving their cultural relations program so any of your contacts in the world of Arts could be very useful introductions for the Embassy team."

When Béatrice suggested that they invite the Heyworths to dinner, it's important to remember Simon had developed a friendly working relationship with Charles Heyworth, the Chargé d'Affaires. Although Simon preferred to keep his career and domestic lives separate, he was comfortable with Charles unlike many of the other senior embassy FSO's. Most were ivy-league educated and Simon felt they looked down on him because of his background and his crippled hand. He had heard references to 'dead hand Luke' and 'culturally crippled' in both Embassies in London and Paris. He ignored them but they hurt. If only these name-callers knew what Simon really did!

Béatrice got on very well with Anna and always enjoyed her company. Anna was a novelist and poet who also ran her own interior design business from their home in Chantilly located about 30 miles from the Embassy. Charles rented a small pied-à-terre during the week so he could get to the Embassy easily.

Surprisingly, the Heyworths insisted that Simon and Béatrice plus their two children came for the weekend to their Chantilly home. Suzanne and Phillipe were still young but the Heyworth children loved playing with them and amusing them. As the taxi approached their Chantilly home, the Montforts were all amazed at the size of the house and the land. "It must be at least 6,000 sq. feet, it's huge. And the land must be 2 acres or more" mentioned Simon. "I wonder what it's like inside?"

"Knowing Anna as well as I do, I'd say it'll be elegant, welcoming but with a dash of modernism" Béatrice opined.

Béatrice was right. As they entered the house they noticed right away the vaulted ceilings, the winding staircase and lush carpeting. Adorning the walls were works of art by famous female French painters of the 20th. Century – Sonia Delaunay who was noted for her use of strong colors and geometric shapes and who, with her husband Robert Delaunay, founded the Orphism movement; the neo-impressionist paintings of Jacqueline Marval; and the avant-garde landscape paintings of Émilie Charmy. "I can't live without my art" Anna said as she briefly described the 10 paintings that were hanging in the vestibule.

"I'm very envious, Anna" admitted Simon "this is the type of art collection I'd like to own one day. Béatrice calls it my pipe dream but who knows, I may surprise everyone."

Anna showed her guests to their bedrooms; king-size with full bathroom-en-suite for the adults and full size beds with bathroom-en-suite for the children.

Over cocktails before dinner Anna explained that her father had bought this house as a vacation home when she was a child; the family all lived in Connecticut where her father's business was based. He admired French culture and wanted his whole family to enjoy the real experience of French life, language and food by spending their vacations in Chantilly. As her father aged the house fell into disrepair; unfortunately his business was forced into bankruptcy due to foreign competition. He made some really bad investment decisions in an attempt to fight his way back and had to declare personal bankruptcy. He asked Charles and Anna if they would like to buy the property and land from him. They negotiated a large loan and bailed out her father who passed away debt-free. They had to extend the loan in order to restore the house and buy the art she loves so much. She laughed "Charles and I will have to carry on working until we are 85 to pay off the capital and interest."

"Oh, but it's so exquisite. I'd love to live in a home like this. Wouldn't you Simon?" asked Béatrice

No I wouldn't he thought to himself. Instead he smiled and replied "Of course. It's delightful. I expect you've done all the interior design yourself Anna – it has your touch?"

"You are very perceptive, Simon. It has taken me, us, ten years to reach this stage. We need another 5 years before the restoration is complete. Oh, I think dinner is ready. Who is hungry? Charles made coq au vin with fresh French bread."

"Sounds delicious Charles. I can't wait to start. I didn't know you were a chef."

Over dinner with Charles and Anna, Simon was very careful to avoid talking about embassy business. Instead they talked about France's opposition to the USA's decision to invade Iraq in 2003 and the wish by certain American politicians to rename 'French fries' as 'freedom fries' in congressional cafeterias. Simon was very opposed to the war commenting "Bush and Cheney just want to prove that they have bigger cojones than Bush Sr. had when he kicked Saddam out of Kuwait but did not finish him off. I don't see any upside for the USA in this war. It will create even more hatred for us than before. The only beneficiaries will be Israel, Iran and the oil companies."

"How do you come to that conclusion?" asked Anna.

"It's simple. Israel will have one less enemy state threatening them with missiles. I'm sure Iraq will have a pro-American government initially. Iran will see an opportunity to spread their Shia power in Iraq once the invasion is over. And oil prices will rocket. And, I forgot, the Kurds will start demanding independence. It will be a complete mess for a long time and I can see that we'll be there for ages. What do you think, Charles?"

"Too complicated for me and way above my pay grade. I'll leave all that to our leaders in DC. But I think freedom fries do sound good..." Charles muttered with a smile but was interrupted by Béatrice who could not believe he had no opinion "but Charles this is so important and will affect so many lives. Surely, you have a point of view. Is it right or wrong to invade a country that has not harmed the USA?"

"Béatrice it's not that simple. We have invaded many countries that have not harmed us. Look at WW2. Germany and Italy had not harmed us. Korea didn't harm us. Vietnam didn't harm us. Need I go on? We have invaded because we want to help and protect our allies. Israel is our strong ally and they clearly welcome the removal of Saddam. Saudi Arabia, Jordan, Egypt, UAE are our allies and would like to see Saddam go."

"But none of the Arab countries will be helping the US will they?" Simon posed. "None of them are prepared to back us militarily."

"You are getting way too serious for a dinner party. I follow what my masters tell me. I'm not a politician, I'm a government official representing the views of our Commander-in-Chief. If he thinks we are under threat from Hussein and that we should invade, I'll trust him and support him. That's it! And I'd advise any other official to do the same. Let's talk about what we are going to do tomorrow. Do you and Béatrice enjoy tennis? We have our own court here. It would be great to have foursome tomorrow morning. What do you say?"

Simon looked at his wife and said "Sounds good but Béatrice will have to serve for me because of my left hand."

"Sure, I forgot. I guess you are limited to just a few sports then Simon" Anna said sympathetically.

"Mainly running – in the summer we run cross country and marathons and in the winter we snowboard and ice skate. I used to swim, snorkel and surf a lot before my accident but those days have gone. Béatrice loves the ocean as I do and has been wonderful in accommodating my deformity so we can both enjoy the same sports and support each other" answered Simon looking lovingly at Béatrice.

"That's just so cute of you two" Anna replied ingratiatingly "I'm sure you will both enjoy the tennis tomorrow. Both Charles and I play regularly at the Chantilly Tennis Club. We've been members for a long time. Charles and I get to meet and entertain many French politicians as well as the elite of French Society there. Oh, that came out wrong. I didn't mean to say that. What I really meant to say was that you can meet the most interesting and influential people at the Club."

Béatrice tried to hide her shock at Anna's snobbishness while Simon smoothly commented "I love meeting those kind of folks as well, Anna. You just never know when they could be helpful to you later in life, do you?"

Anna was not quite sure how to respond to Simon's oblique comment and simply said "Quite true."

Charles had been quietly drinking large balloon glasses of Armagnac while Anna and Simon were discussing sports and he suddenly slurred "Better be off to bed. I'm rather tired. OK for breakfast at 8a with Bloody Marys?"

"I'll pass on the Marys otherwise I'll miss every ball" Simon laughed.

They all wished one another goodnight. Later upstairs in their room Béatrice whispered to Simon "Tennis? We've never played tennis! They will humiliate us. They play all the time."

"Let them. It'll be fun. You never know we may do well. After all we are both fit. Anyway I'm learning so much about Charles. I like him but he's so formal at the Embassy. But here he's a different guy. Boy, does he drink! I can't believe he'll be able to hold a racquet tomorrow let alone hit a ball! Bloody Marys. Who would have thought? "

Béatrice agreed with Simon but then commented "How can they afford their lifestyle. Big house, huge bank loan, all that art – Anna must earn a lot as I doubt Charles earns much more than you."

"I don't know how they make it work. Charles probably earns about $25K more than me a year but after all the high French taxes are deducted I'd guess he might get an extra $12K. As you say Anna must make a good income from her writing and interior design business."

The following morning after breakfast Charles and Anna fortified by several large and strong Bloody Marys played mixed doubles with their guests for about 2 hours. Surprisingly, Simon and Béatrice won one set 8-6 but their hosts won the other sets after several tie-breaks. Charles congratulated his guests on playing so well and suggested "we will meet up around 1p for lunch in Chamonix after we have showered and rested a while. Is that OK?"

"Sure" said Simon. "We'll play some games with the children while you rest."

Simon and his spouse entertained all four children with games of hide-and-seek, dodgeball and Twister while the other adults slept. They all enjoyed a light lunch at a bistro in Chamonix where Simon entertained everybody with his imitation of famous foreign politicians and actors using his formidable linguistic skills. At the same time Simon noticed that Charles was drinking quite heavily.

Anna introduced them to another married couple who arrived as they were all leaving. Charles looked very worried as Anna said "Simon and Béatrice I'd like you meet Monsieur and Madame Fontaine. They are our very dear friends and business partners. Well actually, Monsieur Fontaine was kind enough to loan us sufficient funds to buy my father's house."

Monsieur Fontaine quipped "My dear Anna, you exaggerate. I wasn't being kind. I was being a businessman and a banker. While I'm here I'd like a private word with Charles. Excuse us, please."

While the two men had their private meeting, Anna and Madame Fontaine discussed the latest trends in interior design décor. The children were getting progressively bored while Simon and Béatrice felt awkward so they excused themselves and made their way out of the bistro and went for a short walk. After a few minutes Anna caught up with them saying Charles would be along later.

They didn't see their hosts until dinner. Charles looked very upset and clearly had been drinking heavily all afternoon. Over dinner Anna did most of the talking with Simon and Béatrice making comments and asking a few questions. Eventually, Charles excused himself and went upstairs.

Making sure that he was out of earshot, Simon asked "is Charles OK?

He looks very down."

"Well, he got some really bad news from Fontaine the banker. His business is not doing well in the current economic climate and he needs to call in the large loan he holds on our home as that's his biggest liability. We are both worried. He has given us 3 months to find an alternative lender. Fortunately, Charles does know one other banker who might be willing to take over the loan but the interest rate will be much higher."

"That's unwelcome news indeed, Anna. But before you go that route, have you considered selling and buying a smaller home?" remarked Béatrice cheekily.

"That's impossible. You don't understand. This house is my heritage. My father failed to keep it and I am damn well never going to let it go, whatever it takes. Charles will have to get a better paying career in France so we can take care of the new loan."

That was the end of that discussion! The Montforts retired to bed early as they had to leave promptly the following morning. They happily arrived back at their small apartment in Paris knowing full well they could afford to live there with no ultimatums from bankers.

Some days later at the Embassy Charles apologized to Simon for his impoliteness over the weekend explaining that they had managed to find an alternative source of financing at a much higher rate. At least that would keep Anna happy for the time being. Simon made no comment except to say that he was pleased for them both.

12 MOSCOW 2021

President Gannon's inauguration went well and as indicated by Ambassador Schwarzkopf the President proceeded immediately to roll back the sanctions on Russia, to discontinue arming the anti-Russian Ukrainian freedom fighters and to withdraw the USA from NATO. These executive orders caused uproar in most of Europe; however some European countries who had been sympathetic to Russia for several years were pleased with the US President's decision – Austria, Czech Republic, Hungary and Poland all had governments who were carrying out similar policies to Russia – state control of all TV/Radio stations and media, increased surveillance of 'undesirables' and constant reports of inexplicable 'suicides' of well-known liberals from politics, academia and the arts. People were falling out of windows, falling off bridges, falling out of high-speed vehicles; some were shooting themselves in the back of the head; others were killing themselves with nasty poisons causing long, lingering deaths.

On one recent trip to Austria to meet his agent in Vienna, Simon was shocked to hear from Hans that concentration-like camps had been built in some of the rural parts of Austria to house immigrants, gypsies and non-heterosexuals plus anyone else considered to be subversive by the Government.

Hans had been part of Simon's network from the beginning. Austria had been firmly in the Western Bloc for many years after WW2 but the country was still an excellent center for spying and disinformation since there were so many Russian agents operating in Vienna. Therefore, Simon had decided that having a contact in Vienna was a priority. He came across Hans one afternoon when he was visiting the Jewish Museum in Vienna. Hans was a volunteer and was guiding a small group of tourists through the exhibits; Simon asked if he could join and during a short break they started discussing current affairs in Europe. Hans explained in a very proper but moving way why he enjoyed being a guide "fewer and fewer people in Europe and in the world at large want to know what the Nazis did to the Jews, the Gypsies, and the Slavs. I could go on and list other groups that they tortured and murdered but my job here is to explain to all the visitors what happened to my fellow Jews."

Simon found out that Hans owned a small bank in Vienna – a bank that was used by high-ranking members of the Austrian government and senior staff from the Russian Embassy. Access to politicians and bureaucrats of this caliber was of great interest to Simon who took a risk and commented "you must hear a lot about what's going on or about to happen."

Hans look surprised but remarked that most of the comments he heard was gossip or boring office rumors but there were occasional nuggets that eventually turned out to be true. He looked straight into Simon's eyes saying "I think your government does not appreciate what's happening in Austria. Our government pretends to be neutral but is moving slowly closer to Russia. They have a vast embassy here and have invested heavily in local property and businesses. Our media is becoming very racist and, although I don't feel threatened right now, the past may be repeated."

Listening carefully to Hans' fears for the future, Simon explained why he would be very interested in any information that Hans felt comfortable sharing. Simon felt that he had found a reliable addition for his nascent network.

Now Hans was getting worried being a Jewish banker "Simon, I'm waiting for my front door to be smashed down by a bunch of government thugs who want to drag me and my family off to one of these camps.

"This is exactly what happened to my grandparents and their immediate families when the Nazis came to power. My mother was lucky. She managed to escape to the UK and returned after the War."

"We can get you and your family out, Hans. I'll get our Visa Consul in France to get onto that right away. We can arrange for you to come to the States."

Simon would be sorry to see Hans leave because in the past he had acquired invaluable information about Russia's plans for invading Ukraine and more recently for their removal of the Syrian President al-Assad. "Thank you Simon. I'll give you all the information that your colleague will need. Really I hope I don't have to leave but I must think of my family."

Following the release of the notorious video featuring the Russian President's sexual hypocrisy, he had charged his Intelligence Services to identify the source of the video and all the perpetrators. Today in the Kremlin he had summoned the Heads of the FSB and SVR (Foreign Intelligence Service) to report on their findings. In short, they told him that some terrorists from Chechnya were believed to be the source and had been helped by a western intelligence operator. "Their names and locations?" demanded the arrogant President.

"Ivan Ivanovich, we don't know yet" they reported timidly. "The source we found in the Caucus is still alive after our attempts to extract information from her but she is refusing to share any knowledge of who is behind the plan to dishonor you."

"What about her family? Her friends? Surely you can threaten her that way?"

"Ivan Ivanovich, she has no known family and we have not been able to locate any friends. She has no online presence at all. All we know is that she is a Somali Moslem and is the widow of a former terrorist leader from Ingushetia. She has no children and no family. We eradicated all his family in Ingushetia last year."

"How did you locate this useless woman?"

"Ivan Ivanovich, we received an anonymous call from Albania."

"You got what from where?"

"Ivan Ivanovich, one of my senior officers" explained the Head of the SVR "is related to a member of SHISH (the Albanian Security Service). This person told my officer of the arrival of a lone Somali woman from Ingushetia. He said it was very unusual for such a woman to travel alone into Albania. SHISH tried to monitor her but she managed to evade them until she tried to leave Albania. They stopped her leaving and imprisoned her and then sent her to us in case she had some involvement in the video incident. The Albanian official said "it was a gut feeling."

"Well, let's hope it's not indigestion otherwise you and your colleagues will have been wasting your time. What makes you think a western intelligence operator was involved?"

"Ivan Ivanovich, around the time the Somali woman arrived a so-called businessman from Germany called Erich Schneider came to Tirana. According to SHISH he made several 'sales' presentations to some agricultural consultants and then left the country. He was questioned by SHISH before leaving but was allowed to travel."

"So you've found Erich Schneider?"

"Ivan Ivanovich, he doesn't exist."

"What a surprise! So who you think he is?"

"Ivan Ivanovich, we are assuming he's a member of the German BND (Federal Foreign and Security Service) and we suspect they funded the activity."

"What are you planning to do next?"

"Ivan Ivanovich, we have our own man working in the BND who we hope will identify this spy so we can then interrogate him and eliminate him when he travels abroad again. We prefer not to take action in Germany unless we have to."

"I want to make it very clear to you two that uncovering this plot to dishonor my reputation is your #1 priority – I consider it an act of treason as well as terrorism. Is that clear?"

"Yes, very clear Ivan Ivanovich. We will do our best."

"I don't want your BEST. I want your WORST. Now go. You have seven days to bring either these criminals or your resignations to me."

As the two Heads of Department hurriedly left the President's ornate office, Ivan Ivanovich turned with a contemptuous sneer to his Chief of Staff and barked "make sure you get replacements for those two golovorezy (goons) quickly. Get the Heads of the GRU (Russian Military Intelligence) and Spetsnaz GRU (Russian Special Forces) over here immediately. It's time we stopped playing games with these criminals and caught them."

"Yes immediately Ivan Ivanovich. Do you think it'll be a good idea to ask President Gannon for help? He owes you one as the Americans say."

"Good idea. Get him on the phone."

About half an hour later Ivan Ivanovich was explaining to Steve Gannon what help he needed to catch the perpetrators behind the video debacle. Steve was ready to provide any help his dear friend and political ally wanted; he promised to call the CIA Director and make sure he treated the request with the utmost priority.

The CIA Director couldn't believe what he was hearing as he listened to Steve Gannon's directive. He thought to himself 'WTF are we doing now? Helping some Rooskie tyrant to uncover a takedown that we helped to orchestrate! Gannon is going to be more of a fruitcake than his predecessor'.

As an obedient public official he said "Mr. President, I will ask my top man in Europe to liaise directly with the Russians and provide any help that he thinks is prudent."

Walter took the call from his CIA boss, said very little and contacted Simon with a need-to-talk-now message to his burner phone.

At the same time in the Kremlin, Ivan Ivanovich was meeting with the menacing Heads of the GRU and the Spetsnaz. Their specialty was mass interrogation, mass torture followed by mass slaughter. In that way, they believed, you eradicated everyone likely to be involved even those who were clearly innocent. It was an effective way to instill fear in a population and prevent recurrences of opposition. They both knew the Caucasus well and had a wealth of experience operating there.

"The Americans have promised to help. Their top man in Europe, Walter Talbot, is calling me tomorrow. I shall let him 'soskuchis so mnoy v techeniye neskol'kikh minut' (dick around with me for a few minutes) then tell him he has 24 hours to provide the identity of the perpetrators. After that it's down to you two."

They both smiled and said "Ivan Ivanovich it will be our pleasure to once again round up those backward atheists and teach them a good Russian lesson."

Walter met Simon in a secret location in Paris known only to them. Simon spoke first "I know you are going to speak with the Russian

President tomorrow. I have an idea that will work to deflect his focus away from the damaging video."

"You've got my attention, Simon. What are you proposing?"

"My Russian contact Alexei owes me big time. Also I need to get Dirty Harry off my back. He's insisting that I set up this new network to carry out surveillance on Sunni Moslems in Europe. Alexei likes our video a lot and he knows about Argun and Shali in Chechnya. He'll ask both of them to identify some fake insurgents living in Moscow whom we are going to claim are planning to carry out terrorist attacks on the Kremlin. They will be more than willing to provide Alexei with names of people whom he can frame. He can make sure that incriminating evidence is found by the President's goons. All I need is 72 hours to set it up."

"But what field experience does Alexei have? Won't he be a fish out of water?"

"I doubt it. Before he was rewarded with his current position at the Russian Central Bank, he told me he worked in Cuba as a senior counter-intelligence officer. He knows a lot of people and knows how to persuade them to do what he wants. Alexei has no love for Ivan Ivanovich and would like to see him gone along with all of his oligarchs plus he owes me big time. I have faith in Alexei. He will do what I ask, Walter."

"You have some hold over him then?"

"As I said he owes me. I helped him and his family some time ago to get thru a very bad time. Now is the time to call in a favor."

"OK. I like your logic. Kill two birds with one stone! I'll try and string it out a bit with Ivan Ivanovich but he's not stupid. Make your plan happen. Let's hope it works."

Alexei flew to Paris that same night, had his meeting with Simon and happily agreed to set up the false flag operation. Simon contacted his Ambassador at home and alerted him to the commencement of a joint operation with the Russians to capture terrorist suspects that Simon's network had identified. Unfortunately, Dirty Harry was recovering from a heavy bout of drinking with his card-playing buddies and could only slur a few words "shanku Si. Good news. U and Butriss muss cum over fer dinner shoon."

'At least he was incapable of asking any probing questions' Simon thought thankfully.

Walter called Ivan Ivanovich at the pre-arranged time on a secure video link. As usual the Russian President was dressed in a very expensive suit designed by his favorite tailor in Saville Row, London. "Good to meet you at last, the great Walter Talbot. I've heard a lot about you."

"Good Morning Mr. President, this meeting of ours is somewhat historic. It will usher in a level of cooperation that we have not seen since the days of President Yeltsin and President Clinton or even Premier Stalin and President Roosevelt. I look forward to working with your government and I am grateful for your personal involvement."

"You do not choose good examples of our previous cooperation with the USA. Yeltsin was a drunk who sold the wealth of our motherland to the highest bidder and Stalin was a psychopath who decimated his own people. If you can help identify the criminals who manufactured that fake video, we will be making an excellent first step in re-establishing improved bilateral relations."

Feeling somewhat wrong-footed by Ivan's response, Walter went straight to the point "Mr. President we can help you but in another way...."

"This is not what I agreed with your superior. He assured me that you would be able to identify these criminals. Now you want to change the subject. You are playing games with me, Mr. Talbot. I don't like people who waste my time!"

"I'm not playing games, Mr. President. Please bear with me. I have some news for your ears only – news that is probably more damaging to you and your government than the video."

"OK, go ahead and tell me."

"We have an extremely reliable intelligence source embedded in Moscow who has told us about a major terrorist threat."

"We have threats like this all the time, just like you do in your country. What is so special about this one?"

"This is different. We understand they are going to detonate a series of explosions on the Moscow subway system while your citizens are all returning home to their families. We believe they are amassing enough materiel to kill many hundreds of innocent Muscovites and injure thousands. Such an attack on your society could lead to significant civil unrest and possibly violent protests and demonstrations – actions that you and your government have worked so hard to avoid all these years. Once our source has confirmed all his intel, you will have the opportunity of preventing untold bloodshed in Moscow."

"How do I know you are telling the truth? I need to know all the details now, confirmed or unconfirmed I don't care. You must tell me names, addresses, everything now. I don't want to wait."

"I understand but you know as a former KGB officer we have to ensure that our intelligence is good. You don't want to arrest and interrogate innocent citizens, do you?"

"We do it all the time."

"Regrettably Mr. President we cannot reveal any more details until we have confirmation. And that will take about another 72 hours."

"Not 71 or 73? You are being suspiciously precise."

"OK Mr. President" Walter really wanted to say Mr. Wise-Ass "I'm using a figure of speech."

"A figure of what?"

"*Figura rechi* in Russian, I believe, Mr. President."

"You speak Russian?"

"A little."

"You must come to Moscow and help us interrogate these terrorist when we catch them in 72 hours. You will improve your Russian, I'm sure."

"I'd be delighted so long as my superior allows it. I will be in contact again soon."

"One more thing I wanted to mention to you, Mr. Talbot, please do give my regards to your good friend Simon Montfort in the Embassy and I do hope his new hand will function well. He will have to change his unofficial name from Dead Hand or DH! He does very good cultural work for your country and he travels so much and speaks so many languages so well. We hear so much about him!"

Listening to President Ivan's comments about Simon, Walter didn't know whether to be impressed or worried by Ivan's knowledge of both his own friendship with Simon and Simon's operation on his hand. It sounded like the Russian President was sending a warning message to Simon. Anyway he managed to give an appreciative response to the Russian President's message.

On his return to Paris, Walter sent an encrypted message to Simon confirming that they should proceed. Simon asked Alexei to immediately begin acquiring materiel on the black market in Moscow and to let Argun and Shali know to start lining up potential "terrorists" in Moscow.

In less than 72 hours the plan was ready to put into play. Walter spoke to the Russian authorities and gave the names and addresses of all the suspects they should apprehend. Leaving nothing to chance, the Russians used overwhelming force to make sure that no-one escaped. They had been told of five separate cells comprising a total of fifteen suspects: roads had been closed, cell towers had been switched off and all local radio/TV stations had been banned from broadcasting any programs. With ruthless efficiency all the suspects had been arrested with no shots fired and all the materiel which had been hidden by Alexei's colleagues at the five locations had been captured. Also the security forces "found" various documents detailing stations, times, passenger volumes etc. as well as typed statements from the suspects confirming their plans to cause havoc in Moscow.

The suspects were all driven under heavy security to the FSB Lefortovo Prison in Moscow. There, in the basement, confessions were being extracted from all the prisoners with the promise that since they had not harmed anyone they would not be executed. While this torture was being carried out Ivan spoke directly to the CIA Director in Washington, DC. This conversation was classified but sources within the CIA outlined the conversation as follows:

Russian President: "on behalf of the Russian people I want to express our deep gratitude to you personally for preventing the catastrophe on the Moscow subway system. All the suspects have been interrogated and have admitted their guilt. Their confessions will be reviewed by a special homeland security court in few days and they will be sentenced to hard labor for life in Siberia. Oddly, these terrorists needed little persuasion to admit their guilt. Our interrogators assumed they were novices with little or no experience of mounting a campaign. Anyway, no matter, we captured them and retrieved an arsenal of black-market weapons and explosives. Oddly again, they couldn't explain how they acquired the military hardware. Fortunately, some of the serial numbers had not been removed so it will be easy for us to identify and eradicate that source. The only disappointment I have to report is that Mr. Talbot is not able to help us to find the perpetrators of the malicious fake video falsely portraying me and my colleagues as depraved sexual deviants. If you wish our cooperation to continue I expect the CIA to locate these propagandists."

The CIA Director replied: "Mr. President, it's in both of our great nations' interests to take down terror networks wherever they are. Your success will be a lesson for any future criminals. Our cooperation must remain secret as we don't want to risk exposing our intel source. The video is of great concern to us as well; the widespread use of Artificial Intelligence to generate hoaxes is an increasing problem worldwide and will affect many national leaders. Rest assured we will find the culprits."

After this exchange of diplomatic ambiguity, the CIA Director contacted Walter and Simon and told them about the serial numbers. Simon laughed saying "Alexei had fake serial numbers inscribed on some of the weapons. Anyway he used so many cut-outs that it's downright impossible to trace the weapons back to him."

So everyone was happy! President Gannon had achieved a major milestone in bilateral cooperation with the Russian President; the CIA had demonstrated their ability to work with the Russians; Ambassador Schwarzkopf was delighted with Simon's new anti-Moslem network; Simon was happy to get the Ambassador off his back for a time; Alexei was glad that he had paid his debt to Simon; Argun and Shali had gotten rid of some of their Moslem rivals; but there was one person who had a niggling feeling that he had been duped and that person was Ivan Ivanovich.

Being a former KGB Lieutenant-Colonel, he knew that the majority of these operations rarely proceed so smoothly. Within a few days fifteen terrorists had been detained and fifteen confessions had been signed; a whole cache of weapons had been captured. None of his security services knew anything about these terrorist cells; none of the combatants were known. He felt he had been played and also he sensed that the video had been released by the CIA. He needed an objective opinion and decided to seek an audience with his good friend, His Holiness the Primate of the Russian Orthodox Church – Patriarch Peter.

Like many other former senior officials of the Soviet Communist Empire, Ivan Ivanovich became a fervent "believer" in Orthodox Christianity once the atheism of communism had been swept away. Ivan used the power of religion as yet another lever with which to manipulate the Russian people.

Patriarch Peter was an imposing man with a long, white beard and always wore a vibrant blue set of robes together with a very expensive silver crown. He welcomed Ivan into his sumptuous office that had been equipped with the latest hi-tech equipment imported from the West. The office was furnished in an ornate byzantine style typical of Eastern Orthodoxy but the abundance of wide-screen monitors, computers and surveillance equipment gave the whole area a weird, incongruous affect. The Patriarch offered Ivan some tea from his intricately-designed samovar and asked Ivan what was on his mind. Ivan explained in painstaking detail all the events that had recently unfurled.

The Patriarch listened intently to the President's words, firstly because it was his Christian duty to show empathy and secondly because he relied upon this President to maintain his own elevated status in post-Soviet Russia. Before Ivan Ivanovich became President, the Russian Orthodox Church had little power despite the strong faith of most citizens. Now the Church was held in high esteem and so was the Patriarch. He waited until Ivan had finished and then gave him his humble opinion.

"My son, Ivan Ivanovich, you are a good Orthodox. You know Our

Lord completes His Work on Earth in many different ways, sometimes it is clear what He wants but many times His actions appear obscure. Ivan Ivanovich, the Americans have delivered to you fifteen Islamic terrorists. Was this the work of Our Lord using the CIA as His earthly instrument to help us wage our Holy War against non-believers? You have a choice – take the gift and treat it as His way of protecting Mother Russia or you can scratch away at the itch of your doubts and end up failing to see the enduring value of His gift to you. So what do you say?"

"Your Holiness, your words as always bring delight to my soul. You are right, I did not see this act by the Americans as the work of Our Lord. I now have a direct channel to the Director of the CIA and his Head of Station in Paris. I appreciate your phrase 'enduring value of His gift'. I will leave you now to continue with your important spiritual work."

"Bless you my son, Ivan Ivanovich. Go and protect Mother Russia and make Her stronger than ever before. Remember the famous quotation from Czar Alexander III *'Russia has only two allies – her army and her fleet'*. Now perhaps our Lord is telling you have another ally – the American CIA. But before you leave we must discuss that vile video that was released recently. I know you have refuted it saying it's completely fake. I applaud the way you came down hard on both the public demonstrations and certain misled members of Parliament demanding your impeachment. But you must know, Ivan Ivanovich, that many good Russians still believe the propaganda. If you permit me I should like to draw a similarity here between the Kremlin's reaction to the video and the Vatican's reaction to the charges of priestly pedophilia."

Ivan Ivanovich's cheeks were about to burst. 'How dare this old fool compare me to bunch of gay pederasts? I, the President of all of Mother Russia did not seek this idiot's counsel so I could be vilified'. Ivan was on the point of bellowing at the Patriarch but his intuition counseled him to keep his mouth shut. The Patriarch continued "the result of the Vatican's hesitation to face the truth was a worldwide loss of respect and faith. Now they are having to slog away at rebuilding that trust. You must not go down that path, Ivan Ivanovich. Since you became President, maybe Emperor one day, you have done much good for the Motherland – good that you don't want to see evaporate. My advice is that you must put this shameful event to bed forever otherwise some of your citizens will continue to believe the lies that the crowd-pleasing western press want to publish.'

Ivan raised his head slowly to look at the Patriarch and decided to appear thoughtful thinking 'I really do like the idea of Emperor of Russia'. He thanked the Patriarch for his insight and advice. He didn't care what the western media said about him and he didn't care what a few backward, vodka-swilling people living in poor rural villages like Batagan or Severolym or wherever said or thought about him in secret. He ruled parliament, the media and all the cities with an iron fist – that's what counted!

At the end of their meeting Ivan thought that the old dotard with the long, white beard had been by and large quite useful. He felt happier now, much less suspicious about the CIA's involvement in unravelling the terror plot. He would, however, continue with his plan to take down the CIA spymaster working in Paris. Turning the spy into a double agent working for Russia would be an even better result. Ivan's personal intelligence network had already established a reliable contact in Paris to help him execute this plan.

The Patriarch was no dotard. All his predecessors since the times of St. Peter (Metropolitan of Russia from 1308 thru 1326) had to counsel rulers of Russia who lied, cheated and slaughtered their way to power. They had to listen to the same tales of sorrow, hypocrisy and self-justification that this Patriarch had just experienced with the current Russian President. 'Nothing is new, it's the same old stuff dressed in new clothes' he mused to himself. I have to keep Ivan happy though, so I can keep my own power base and influence,

· **God willing!'**

13 BAD LUCK ALWAYS COMES IN THREES

The next night following the arrests in Moscow, Simon was busy preparing dinner in their apartment without feeling any guilt about the fifteen innocent Moslems he had sacrificed. Watching Simon happily getting their meal ready, Béatrice remarked to Simon that he looked less stressed than he had been recently. "Do I? I guess affairs at the Embassy have calmed down a bit. Dirty Harry is less demanding and much less obnoxious. In fact he's going to invite us to have dinner along with the Heyworths and Talbots at his residence next week. I'm waiting for the exact day. Since you aren't touring so much now, you can come and enjoy the fun with me."

"But of course. I'm looking forward to meeting your new boss and his wife."

"He'll like you I'm sure. I just hope he keeps his hands to himself and controls his drinking. Hopefully his wife will have him on a short leash."

Béatrice was gregarious and had a very warm personality that everyone liked, especially men. When she used to tour at lot throughout Europe, Simon had complete faith in her fidelity. He knew that in her world, many musicians and artists were far more tactile than professionals in other walks of life where such behavior was discouraged for fear of allegations of abuse. Many of her male contemporaries (gay and straight) were far more likely to share and explore feelings and emotions rather discuss politics, investments or sport. Some of these men were Beatrice's close personal friends. Simon accepted that was the way of the world of music.

"I wonder when Suzanne will be calling us about her career interview in Italy" Béatrice asked as she was enjoying Simon's excellent dish of medallions of pork, pureed potatoes and mange tout peas sautéed in onions, garlic and ginger. Suzanne had told her parents a few days before that she had applied for a team lead position with the #1 Italian fashion house at their new head office in Milan.

As if Suzanne had heard her mother's question, Beatrice's mobile rang displaying her daughter's ID.

"Hello mignonne, how are you? How did the interview go?"

"Mama, I'm in jail in Monaco. After the interview I went with some friends to a casino in Monaco and I've been arrested for assaulting a security guard. I can bail myself out but I need an attorney. The local Press are waiting outside because the police or someone told them the daughter of an American diplomat is in jail. Justin Heyworth was with me at the casino."

"Oh, that's awful. Your father can help. Wait a minute."

Simon would want to know exactly what happened. He had no idea that Suzanne liked to gamble.

"Papa, I'm so sorry about this. I know it will reflect badly on you once the national Press hear about it."

"That's unfortunate. Are you OK? Were you hurt? Tell me exactly what happened? Why was the Heyworth's son, Justin, with you?"

"So many questions, Papa. I'll give you the short version. I gamble, OK, and I'm very good at it. I got offered the job in Milan and to celebrate I went to Monaco where I have some friends. We all went to the Casino Monaco. Justin asked me out recently (bit of a surprise since I don't know him very well) and I told him I was busy traveling. Later he texted me asking where I was so I told him about the casino. He met me and my friends there yesterday. Anyway, I started winning at my favorite card game, vingt-et-un. You remember you me taught that game when I was a child."

"Yes, I remember but for fun not playing for real and getting arrested!"

"Sure, but I love the buzz. So I was up about $20,000.00 and....."

"How much?"

"$20K. Two security guards came up to me and told me to cash in my winnings and leave immediately. It was so embarrassing. My friends left the table but Justin went up to one of the guards and said something. Next second this guard got hold of my arms and started pushing me towards the cashier desk. I told him to release his grip as he was hurting me. He didn't so I tripped him up and hit him hard on the chin. Knocked him out completely."

"Oh dear Suzanne. How awful! Well he deserved it and I'm glad you remembered your self-defense lessons. What happened next?"

"Coming to that. The casino called the police. When they arrived, Justin got all antsy saying 'she has diplomatic immunity, she's the daughter of an American diplomat in Paris.' The police said that would have to be sorted out later but right now I was under arrest. I am now in a smelly cell on Rue Suffren-Reymond waiting for my bail hearing tomorrow morning. I can cover my bail but I need an attorney to prosecute the casino and their guard plus handle the Press."

"I'll have Marc Reynaud fly down to see you immediately. He'll sort all this out. Maman says she will be with you tomorrow. I have to stay at Embassy."

"I'm also worried about my new career. Once the news is out in the European Press about my arrest, they may decline to confirm the offer. Also I have already resigned my job in Paris. So I could be unemployed. If that happens I want compensation."

"Quite right. You need to contact the Milan fashion house as soon as possible and get ahead of the story. Tell them you were assaulted and you are suing the casino. But talk to Marc first. I need to contact him at home and ask him to get on a plane tonight. I'm going to give the phone to Maman now."

Simon called Marc and he agreed to fly down to Monaco and visit Suzanne first thing in the morning.

After Béatrice finished her call with her daughter, Simon exploded "what does she think she's doing – gambling, hitting a security guard, getting thrown in jail and involving the Press. This is not good for my career. This is exactly what Dirty Harry wants – an excuse to get rid of me. I can just imagine the headlines in the popular press – **Attaché's Daughter in Undiplomatic Fight** and **Diplomat's Daughter Loses it at Casino.** "

"My God Simon! She is your daughter. She needs your help not your blame. Shame on you! She didn't involve the Press. It was Justin and his big mouth. You need to get hold of Charles and ask him to tell his son to keep his mouth shut."

Simon explained "You just don't comprehend how tenuous my position is. Like all government employees I will be called before the Purity Committee in DC. So far 35% of our staff at the Embassy have been terminated for infringement, real or alleged, of the new purity laws passed by Congress. Suzanne's actions could lead to my dismissal. That means I have to return to the USA as I'm not a French citizen, you and our children will have to remain here in France as none of you are US Citizens."

"Simon there's no need to be so pessimistic. Even if you are dismissed surely you can get a visa from the French government to remain in France until you can become a citizen? After all, you've been married to a French citizen for over 20 years."

"You are so positive Béatrice. I love that about you. I'll have to check that out just in case."

"So who has been dismissed so far?"

"Lower level grade personnel mainly. Unfortunately one of my able assistants was among them. Eric had been having a sexual liaison with the Cultural Attaché in the UK Embassy. The Purity Committee didn't approve saying that gay relationships bring disrepute to the Department of State. The fact that he was very loyal, capable and hard-working didn't count. I and my colleagues wrote letters of support to all members of the Committee outlining his skills and achievements, but they were ignored. Even Dirty Harry stepped in and tried to help. Thank goodness Stephanie is not affected – she's French."

Béatrice told him "It's getting late. I know you'll have a heavy day tomorrow. You had better get some sleep. I'll book my flights to Monaco now."

Meanwhile the Deutsche Post in Germany was flying overnight from Berlin a postcard for Simon which would arrive unexpectedly at his apartment early the following day. This postcard would remain in his mailbox until he returned home late that night.

Béatrice arrived at the jail mid-morning and took Suzanne away once she had paid the bail of $10,000.00. A trial date in 2 weeks had been booked. The three of them including their family attorney Marc Reynaud sat in a local coffee shop and discussed developments since the previous night.

Marc had been the Montfort's family attorney for several years. He had a kind face and spoke to them reassuringly. "I discussed Suzanne's case with the local prosecutor. Fortunately we both attended the Paris Law School and we were good friends – played a lot of tennis, partied, skied and so on. He's not going to play hard ball. If Suzanne takes a plea deal, she'll get a small fine. If she opts to go to trial and she's found guilty, she will have to serve a short sentence at the Remand Prison of Monaco. However, in her defense, Suzanne maintains that the security guard made an unprovoked assault and she broke free after he refused to let her go. He had no authority to manhandle her like he did. Her friends cannot corroborate her version of events and neither can any other gamblers. The only person who can help her is Justin Heyworth who has disappeared and is not responding to calls or texts. I've called Simon and he should have finished speaking with Charles Heyworth. Let's put him on speakerphone now."

Simon was taking a light lunch with Walter Talbot at one of their "secret" restaurants tucked away in a quiet street. They were discussing the Moscow take-down and Suzanne's arrest. He recognized Marc's ID and updated him on his conversation with Charles.

"Well, Charles wasn't very helpful. He claims he had no idea that his son was in Monaco and he is unable to reach him. Justin's employer mentioned that he was taking a two week vacation. I'm working on a couple of other avenues and if I have success I'll get back to you, Marc."

Turning to Walter, Simon opened his hands like a supplicant and said "I need your help to find Justin Heyworth. I have the feeling that Charles might be protecting him. What can you do?"

"I'll ask one of my contacts at the Sûreté to put out a BOLO for him. Do you have a description, photo?"

"No problem. I have plenty of photos of our two families on my phone. Choose what you want and I'll send you them now. He lives with his parents in Chamonix and works at the BNP Paribas which is located on the Blvd. des Italiens."

In a few minutes later Simon received another call from Marc stating that Suzanne was definitely going to sue the security guard, the security company and the casino. He confirmed that Suzanne had talked to her new employer in Milan and had explained the situation before the popular press published their usual salacious headlines. Fortunately, the Milan fashion house had agreed not to rescind their employment offer but had inserted a probationary period of 6 months in Suzanne's contract. Suzanne was OK with that deal, he said. So it was down to Simon to find Justin.

"I'm on it" Simon assured him.

Simon got back to their apartment before Beatrice and Suzanne arrived. He found the postcard in a sealed envelope with his name and address written in a familiar style. It featured a photo of the Berlin Wall at AlexanderPlatz in its final days. Amira had written the following words-

Du hast geholfen, die Mauer niederzureißen, und dann hast du mir das Herz gebrochen.

You helped break down the Wall and then you broke my heart.

"Amira, what game are you playing with me" Simon cried out to an empty room. Simon was very puzzled by these cryptic cards after so many years of zero contact. It was over thirty years since they had seen each other in Berlin after his accident at the Wall. Is she looking for revenge after such a long time? Surely not! Did she want something from him? If that was the case, then she would have given him some means of getting back in touch with her. He felt very uneasy even threatened by the two cards that he had received.

Little did Simon know that there would be a third postcard sent to his office where all the incoming mail was inspected and read due to their security protocols. At least three Embassy personnel would read that postcard before it arrived on his desk. And it would prove the most damaging to his career and eventually his marriage.

The next morning Simon got a call from Walter confirming that his contacts at the Sûreté had located Justin Heyworth. He had been spotted in a restaurant with an older man and the two detectives had followed them back to an apartment. They had arrested him and charged him with obstruction of justice; at the same time the Monaco police had inspected the casino's security cameras confirming that Justin did speak with one of the guards and then he clearly watched the guard manhandling Suzanne. The local police in Monaco said that they had received too many complaints about the casino's behavior and were treating the assault on Suzanne seriously. Justin would be flown to Monaco later today and be up before a magistrate tomorrow.

Both Suzanne and Béatrice were relieved with Simon's news. They wanted to know how Simon had found Justin. "I called in a favor from a friend, that's all" was Simon's response. "It's looking much better now. You still have your new career in Milan. I reckon the Monaco prosecutor will drop the charges against you. Marc will continue to sue the casino, the security company and the guard. Justin will probably get a fine. What I don't understand is why he did all this. I'm not going to discuss it with his father as I don't want Charles to know anything about my involvement in tracking Justin down. That stays in the family, OK? I have to get to the Embassy now. See you both later?"

Suzanne said she would like to stay for a few days with her parents and see her brother Phillipe before she went to Milan. She thanked her 'papa' and 'maman' profusely for all their help. "That's what parents do" Simon said generously. Remembering his anger when he first learnt about Suzanne's arrest, Béatrice was somewhat annoyed by her husband's hypocrisy. "I didn't realize you could be so two-faced' she thought. Suddenly Simon's new hand started throbbing and then went into a painful spasm. Béatrice noticed Simon was holding his left hand and was grimacing thru clenched teeth.

"What's wrong?" she asked.

"I don't know. It's never happened before. But it's wearing off now, thank goodness. It felt like a hot knife was piercing my skin. If it happens again I'll have to check with Guy. I'm returning to the Embassy." Kissing his wife and daughter au revoir, he left their apartment and walked quickly to the nearby Metro station wondering what had happened to his new forearm and hand.

Arriving at the Embassy in about 30 minutes, Simon thought that Stephanie looked very agitated saying that she had something very important to show Simon. They walked to his new small office which had been downsized with the arrival of the new Ambassador and had been downsized again following the dismissal of his assistant Eric. The office was now a cramped space in the basement, the size of a large utility closet. But it was quiet and remote so not many people bothered Simon which allowed him to continue with his clandestine work uninterrupted. Stephanie handed him an envelope which had been opened. He immediately recognized the handwriting as belonging to Amira. Before he removed the postcard he asked Stephanie "how any employees have read the card?"

"Security, the Ambassador's secretary and Mr. Heyworth" she replied.

"That means by now half the Embassy knows its contents" Simon calculated. Stephanie tried to mollify his concerns saying "I doubt it, Simon, as it's written in Russian with no translation."

"That helps but it's easy to scan it thru a web translator. Anyway I had better read it. You can stay while I go thru it."

Stephanie waited patiently while Simon stared intently at the photo. The picture was the photo the elderly English couple took of Simon and Amira at the Kremlin War Memorial in 1989. Amira had written the following text:

Perestroika i glasnost' razzhigali vozrozhdeniye natsii, v to vremya kak ya s trepetom smotrel na novuyu zhizn', kotoraya iskhodila ot menya cherez tebya.

Perestroika and Glasnost kindled the rebirth of a nation while I gazed in awe at the new life that came from me thru you.

"It sounds very poetic but what does it mean?" asked Stephanie.

Simon replied angrily "The writer is someone I knew thirty years ago. She's lying saying I have a child by her. The Purity Committee in the US will love this, Stephanie."

"Oh yes, I forgot to tell you that the meeting with the Committee has been scheduled for the fifteenth of next month."

"Thanks Stephanie. I need to make some calls now."

Simon made one call and that was to set up a meeting with Walter in the Tuileries

Garden near the Place de la Concorde and the Louvre. Simon suspected he was being framed ahead of the Purity Committee meeting in DC. Somehow Suzanne, Amira and Justin were all involved, wittingly or unwittingly, in this plot to dishonor him. He wanted to run all his suspicions by Walter to make sure he was being logical. After that meeting he planned to sit down with Béatrice and tell her everything about his past and his real role at the Embassy.

It was a beautiful afternoon in the Tuileries. The Garden dates back to 1564 when it was created by Catherine de' Medici following the accidental death of her husband Henry II. It became a public park after the French Revolution. Simon arrived early checking to make sure that he was not being followed – Dirty Harry had been very pleasant to him since the Moscow takedown but he didn't trust him.

He spotted Walter sitting on a bench nonchalantly reading his notebook and eating a Jambon-Beurre for his lunch. Seeing Simon approaching he got up, smiled and said "let's take a walk towards the Jeu de Paume. It's not so crowded over there. So what's on your mind, Simon? I can't believe the weather. I doubt though you have good news for me. You look too serious."

"You read me too well, my friend. But first, let me thank you for your help in getting Justin Heyworth apprehended. His father hasn't mentioned it all to me so I'm OK with that for the time being. My family will not discuss my role in that arrest and they have no idea of your involvement. Justin has been charged in Monaco and is still in jail waiting for his father to bail him out. I know the

Heyworths have a lot of liquidity issues so Justin might be spending some time there. Suzanne's attorney reckons that Justin will admit that he saw the guard molest my daughter as a plea deal but he can't remember what he said exactly to the guard that made him be so aggressive. At the end of the day so long as Suzanne is cleared of all charges and wins her lawsuit, I don't care what happens to Justin." "Glad to help but I suspect you have something more complex to share with me."

Simon replied "I do and let's keep walking. Here's the issue I'm dealing with." He told Walter about the three postcards and their inscriptions with the last one implying that Amira had given birth to their child. He explained to Walter his belief that Justin had been part of a plan to embarrass Simon by getting his daughter arrested for assault. The postcards and the arrest would probably be raised by the Purity Committee and treated as grounds for his dismissal for bringing shame on the Foreign Service.

"If you take the attempt to incriminate my daughter and the arrival of these postcards and then add Ivan Ivanovich's comments made to you about me, then I suspect there is a plan to bring me and my network down. I expect there's already a clandestine operation in place in Paris or even the Embassy. I must say it's a brilliant strategy to manipulate your enemy to destroy itself and their own creation."

"Well as you know I'm no admirer of conspiracy theorists but I can't fault your instincts Simon. I have known you too long. It is hard for me to be the devil's advocate and shoot holes in your theory. So what's your counter strategy?"

Simon was ready with his response. "Well first I must tell Béatrice everything. It's so involved and inter-linked she needs to know it all otherwise she won't grasp its importance. It will be hard for her to hear that I've been kind of deceiving her for over 20 years. Then I'm flying to Budapest to see an old friend of mine. I need to track Amira down and establish why she's sending me these cards. That may lead me to who's running the operation in Paris. "

"That's dangerous but I can understand why you would want to do that. Once Béatrice knows everything, you may have to cease operating as a spy, Simon. National Security – she has no clearance. Anyway good luck and let me know how I can help. See you and Beatrice at the Ambassador's residence tomorrow. "

Simon had forgotten about that dinner invitation so he texted his spouse to remind her.

"Looking forward to it. R U?" was her reply.

Not all he thought and especially afterwards when I am going to tell you about Amira etc.

The following evening at the Ambassador's residence which was located in a very fashionable part of Paris along the Rue Faubourg St. Honoré, Simon was expecting to see the Heyworths and Talbots. He was looking forward to watching how Charles would behave following his son's arrest. Simon had not seen Charles at the Embassy as he had taken some last-minute vacation since the incident in Monaco.

Dirty Harry was in good form greeting them warmly in the huge entrance to the mansion. His wife, Daphne, asked if they would like a tour before they had cocktails. Both Simon and Charles politely excused themselves having been round the residence many times before and instead sat in sumptuous chairs in the sunroom.

Charles spoke first apologizing for Justin's embarrassing behavior. "I don't know what made him act like that. It was so unlike him. Somehow the police in Paris found him and arrested him; we spent some time in Monaco helping him get thru the trial. How is Suzanne doing?"

"She's well. Glad that it's all over and she's in the clear. Wants to concentrate on her career in Milan now. Don't think she'll be visiting casinos anytime soon."

"I heard that she's suing the security company and the casino. How long will that take to get to court? Will Justin be involved?"

"I have no idea Charles. It's a civil case and as you know there's a huge backlog. They keep going on strike!"

"I only ask because Justin is quite frail. Courts, police and jail all frighten him."

"He used to be very outgoing and confident. What happened?"

"I don't really know. The only change we've noticed is that since he left college and joined Paribas Bank he has become very withdrawn. It could be his job or it could be his new friend. He won't tell us much about him except that he's a bit older than Justin and is now unemployed. He lost his job recently. They share an apartment. That's where he was arrested. Both Anna and I are very worried. We've been round to his apartment but either no-one's there or they are not opening the door to us. He won't reply to our phone calls or texts. At least we were able to spend some time with him in Monaco. The trouble was he had hardly anything to say and as soon as our flight got us back to Paris he ran off and got the Metro back to his home. Didn't thank us or anything."

As Charles recounted his story, Simon noticed that tears began to roll down his cheeks. Suddenly Charles looked very haunted as if he were somewhere else. Simon placed his hand on his colleague's shoulder and commiserated with him. "Would you like to know more about his friend and see if that is the reason why he has changed so much?"

"Yes we would but how can you do that? What would you do?"

"I have to travel to Budapest for a few days on business but when I return I'll let you know how I can help. OK?"

"You don't know how much that would mean to us, Simon. We would be most grateful." Charles actually smiled and looked more like his normal self.

As the tour had finished, Dirty Harry announced that cocktails were being served in the Dining Room. Everyone gathered there and enjoyed the polite chit-chat that always happens before more serious conversations take place. Simon was watching the Ambassador, surreptitiously wondering whether he could be undermining him and his spy network. But how would he know Amira? Enough of this speculation he thought and changed his gaze to watch his wife charm the Ambassador's spouse, Daphne, as she praised the beautiful décor in their residence. What she didn't see was Anna Heyworth's look of disdain at her compliments. To be honest the Heyworth's home was far more tastefully furnished than the Residence – it was too old and heavy. Regrettably, the Department of State's budget didn't extend to modernization upgrades. Simon was not looking forward to telling Béatrice all his secrets later that evening. It could be a long time before he might see his wife so happy! And that made him very sad.

Daphne asked all her guests to take a seat at the table as dinner was ready. She announced that the meal had been prepared by the Embassy chef Jean Claude but that she had chosen the dishes. She asked all the men to change seats to their left after each course so that all the guests could mingle. Everyone smiled politely but some of them thought that was slightly pretentious as they all knew each other. Anyway the men did as she requested.

Before they sat down Walter murmured a question to Simon "Have you told Béatrice yet?"

"No, I will later tonight."

They continued talking at the table but focused on the political situation in the US. Walter explained how his meeting with the Purity Committee went; he was careful not to bore everyone and share the details of all the questions and his answers but just described the process. The hearing had lasted four hours and was live streamed as none of the questions concerned his CIA work; the three-man committee focused entirely on his private life – his time in France with Simon and John, his premarital relationships, his marriage, his financial situation, his children, his religious beliefs and so on. As he spoke more and more Simon noticed he was becoming quite agitated; rarely had he seen Walter so annoyed, he was always so laid-back. Walter complained quite loudly "it was a gross invasion of my privacy, it was most embarrassing to be sitting there as if I were on trial." Eventually his wife, Mary, intervened saying with a smile "Wally, you are drowning out everybody else's conversation." Walter apologized and was astonished to hear the Ambassador comment that the Purity Committee inquiry was "clearly a very painful but necessary experience. Fortunately, I was granted an exemption as I'm not an employee but a contractor." Simon nearly choked on his consommé when he heard Dirty Harry's words. How come a known molester gets a free pass, he wondered?

Picking up the Ambassador's words with care, Simon asked him "how does that work, being a contractor? Do you receive standard

Federal benefits and diplomatic immunity like the rest of us, Harry?"

"I get the immunity like you do but no benefits. I get an extra tax-free allowance instead. You see, I've never been a Federal Employee. Two or so years ago I was asked to become Ambassador to the UK and then here. I still have my job open in the oil industry if things don't work out here. I'm in good shape" he boasted. His plump cheeks were beginning to glow from the many glasses of fine Burgundy he had been drinking during the gourmet entrée of pheasant roasted in calvados, accompanied by apples, aubergines au gratin and spinach soufflé.

Turning to Walter's spouse, Mary, the Ambassador started quizzing her about her career making rather stupid comments like 'I bet you don't have to be careful with what you say like Walter has to'. Before she could attempt a response, the seemingly-demure Mary went into complete anaphylactic shock gasping for air and clutching her throat. Walter leapt towards her grabbing her purse off the floor and removed an Epinephrine injector. He expertly applied the live-saving chemical into her thigh and carried her carefully towards a couch.

The Ambassador's wife felt awful and was utterly speechless for a few minutes. Dirty Harry was so wasted that he had no idea what was happening. He probably thought that Mary wanted a short rest. Simon asked "does Mary need an ambulance?" Walter's reply was understandably brief "Yes. Although the drug works well, she'll need to be checked by a physician."

The ambulance arrived quickly and took Walter and Mary to the hospital. Daphne was upset saying "no-one told me that she was allergic." Her husband had fallen asleep at the table and was snoring stertorously. So Charles and Simon along with their wives said it would be best if they excused themselves and left early.

Driving back to their apartment Simon and Béatrice discussed Mary's distressing attack. "I'm so glad Mary brought her own food when they dined with us. She could've died if Walter hadn't got to her so quickly."

Simon replied "I guess neither of them let the Ambassador's staff know that she's allergic to certain foods. And she didn't check with Daphne before she started eating. I really don't know how the two of them could forget to mention it."

Simon cast his mind back to dining with the Talbots. Mary never ate at restaurants. At home she would insist on preparing all her own meals, never letting anyone including Walter help her. When dining at friends' homes like the Montforts, Mary would bring all her own food and beverages and also all her own silverware and flatware. She was afraid of any cross-contamination. In addition to coping with her food allergies, she was mildly bipolar and suffered from OCD. She refused to take any medication to alleviate these disorders because "I don't want any chemical poisons in my body". Because she was so careful with her food and so much of her energy was consumed by her twin disorders, she had a very slim figure. Charles had quietly mentioned several times to Simon how attractive Mary was. Simon didn't disagree but he kept thinking that she reminded him of someone else.

Walter clearly doted on Mary because she constantly told everyone how supportive and understanding he was. He never complained to Simon nor for that matter to anyone else as far as Simon could tell. Only once did he make a comment to Simon about her condition saying "I have managed to persuade Mary to join a support group and to take therapy classes to try and help her disorders." Conversing with Mary was not easy. She would not look at you when she spoke and she delivered her words in a semi-robotic manner with a slight mid-European accent.

Arriving back at their apartment Simon sat down with Béatrice and holding her hand he said he had some very important information to share with her about his past and how it had been affecting his career. She was very worried because she had never seen Simon so serious. Fortunately, Suzanne was out seeing her brother and would be back late.

Simon told her about Amira, how they met and their travels to Berlin and Moscow in the late 80's. He explained how their relationship ended with his accident at the Berlin Wall and his decision to return home to the USA. Then out of the blue over a period of a few months he received postcards from her.

"Why didn't you tell me about the first card?" she asked.

"I just didn't think it was that important. It wasn't threatening in tone, it was just a photo of Chamonix scenery that I liked- it was truly 'my favorite spot'. But when Suzanne was assaulted, then the other cards started to arrive and then the Purity Committee issued their schedule of hearings – I started putting things together. There's also something else you need to know. It concerns my career at the Embassy. I wear two hats – Cultural Attaché is my official role but for many years I have been running a spy network out of the Embassy."

Béatrice collapsed in laughter saying "Simon, have you been drinking? You've been reading too many spy novels. Oh Mon Dieu you aren't joking are you? I can see in your face that you are telling the truth. You've been spying for years! You could have been killed! That's why Suzanne was assaulted. Are you crazy? It could have been much worse. Who is going to be next – Phillipe or me or you? Why have you been doing this kind of work?" she cried out with tears rolling down her youthful cheeks.

Simon tried to console her but she pushed him away. "Leave me alone. I can't talk to you right now. Give me time to process all of this then we can talk. I'm going out for a walk. Just tell me who knows what you really do. Oh I've just realized why you accompanied me or met me on many of my orchestral tours in Europe – you were selecting agents for your network. You've not only deceived me but you've used me! In fact, it's worse than that – you married me so that you could get access to potential agents. And now this woman from your past is telling you that you have a 30 year old child."

Simon meekly replied "The Ambassador and Walter Talbot know. No-one else knows in Europe. At least no-one else should know in Europe. I'm truly sorry I've upset you, Béatrice, and I will make it up to you in any way I can."

With that Béatrice slammed the apartment door and didn't return until late the following day. Simon found out later that she had stayed with a friend of hers from the orchestra.

After a restless night sleeping alone, Simon returned to the Embassy the following morning. Although he didn't feel at all like working he had to help Stephanie add some finishing touches to one or two major cultural events that she and Eric had been working on. Stephanie would be overloaded with work until the Ambassador allowed a replacement for Eric so Simon wanted to help as much as he could before he left for Budapest and the USA.

Later that day he returned home to the apartment and found both Béatrice and Suzanne there. Hoping that Béatrice had not been discussing his covert role with their daughter, he walked into the kitchen and heard these words "he has to stop this work." Fearing the worst he greeted both of them and asked whether they would like to dine out tonight. Béatrice appeared worn-out and looking at her daughter said "Suzanne is going back to her apartment now and I'd prefer to stay here. You can go out and eat by yourself if you prefer."

"No thanks. I'm staying here and I'll fix something for both of us. When do you leave for Milan, Suzanne?"

"Early tomorrow."

"OK. We'd like to take you to the airport wouldn't we?"

"Maman is doing that. I'm sure you have plenty of things to do at the Embassy."

Well, thought Simon, this is not going so well. He kissed his daughter goodbye, wished her well with the lawsuits and then walked away to take a shower.

Once Suzanne had left, Simon broached the thorny subject of his work saying "I guess you've had time to think thru what I told you the other night. I really meant what I said. You and our children mean everything to me and I will do whatever you want to change things."

Béatrice looked angrily at Simon saying "Yes, I've had plenty of time to think. You have hurt me deeply. Right now I cannot forgive you. You can't go back and undo your past. I don't really care whether you are a spy or not. It's up to you. I'd prefer you did not live here for the time being. Forget about preparing a meal. Use your time to pack and go."

"I won't be doing that, Béatrice. This is my home as much as it is your home. If you are not comfortable with me here, you ought to find a temporary alternative. Anyway I'm flying to Budapest tomorrow for a few days. Then I may to travel elsewhere before my trip to the States so you'll have plenty of time alone here to think about our marriage. Before I answer all the prying questions that the Purity Committee will ask, I have to find out why Amira sent those postcards, that's the reason I'm traveling to Budapest. I will have to confront her to find out the truth. That won't be pleasant."

Béatrice looked at him with those silver-grey eyes that aroused such love in his heart and spoke dispassionately to him "You have to do what is necessary, Simon. Travel safe."

Next morning Simon struggled to get off the couch in the lounge. He hadn't slept well and felt really miserable. Despite all the stress he had been thru the past few days, his new hand felt great. No spasms and no pain. Simon wondered what had caused the problem he'd experienced the other day when he was outwardly sympathetic to Suzanne's problems but he was raging inside. "Perhaps my hand is telling me when I'm being hypocritical, or overly diplomatic or even lying. Boy, I must call Guy when I return and get his input. He'll probably blame the drugs."

He had an early flight to catch so he could visit his agent in Budapest. He didn't feel like traveling at all. He couldn't believe his marriage could be ending. But he had to solve the mystery behind the postcards.

As he waited in the Charles De Gaulle departure lounge, Simon called his son knowing that he was an early riser. He wanted to find out more about Justin. Phillipe and he had been quite close when they were younger – there was just a few years difference between, Justin being slightly older. Since Philippe was such a gentle person, Justin had taken him under his wing and had treated him like a younger brother. They enjoyed each other's company and got on very well. Simon asked his son how his studies in speech pathology were progressing and then moved onto Justin. "I'd like to chat with you about Justin. Have you heard from him recently? He's been in a bit of trouble lately, you may have heard about that from Suzanne."

"She told me about the incident. But it's strange you should ask me about him, Papa. Because he called me two days ago, saying that he felt so ashamed about what had happened to Suzanne. He sounded very upset on the phone, crying all the time, saying it really wasn't his fault. So I asked him whose fault was it then. He said he was made to do it."

"Interesting. Did he say who did that?"

"No. I asked but he wouldn't tell. He said he's very afraid. Of what? I asked. Of someone close to him - was all he said."

"Did he talk about any new friends he has?"

"Real briefly. I don't know why he called me but he suddenly broke off saying he had to go because Eric was back. Do you want me to go and visit him and find out more?"

With Béatrice's fears about their family being at risk, he advised Philippe "there's no need to do that. Justin clearly has some problems. I'm not sure what they are. It's better if I let Charles know and see if he can help his son. If Justin calls you again, just listen to what he says like a good friend and then call me. OK?"

"You can rely on me, Papa."

"I know I can. Love you. Au revoir."

Joseph Erdész had been Simon's agent for many years in Hungary. To help find the right person as his agent, Simon had enlisted the help of a close friend and fellow officer at the US Embassy in Budapest explaining that he was working clandestinely as an undercover CIA officer.

His friend was very surprised warning Simon that this type of work, while at first glance may appear exciting, could compromise his role as a diplomat. Simon ignored his friend's counsel and persuaded him to recommend several potential sources whom Simon investigated thoroughly. Eventually, Simon's friend did admit that their Embassy had a similar situation where one of their diplomats was an intelligence officer keeping an eye on the activities of the Hungarian Constitution Protection Office because its internal security agents enjoyed very close relationships with their Russian counterparts.

Over the course of a few days Simon and his friend casually met these potential sources at local bars and restaurants so Embassy staff wouldn't find out. Simon was introduced as an "anonymous American businessman working in Paris" interested in making considerable strategic investments in the Hungarian economy. (Not too far from the truth!) Simon was immediately impressed by Joseph and met him again alone and revealed the real purpose behind the meetings. Joseph was delighted and described to Simon how his background would be such a good fit.

"I was a member of several liberal democratic governments that Hungary enjoyed after the collapse of Communism. But, as you know, in 2010 a populist right-wing party was elected and has been in power until today. I retired from active politics following the defeat of my party again in 2014. Although remote from the day-to-day activities of government, I still have many contacts and friends in the bureaucracy, some of whom do not approve of the extreme policies that these new politicians are planning. Because of my consulting business, I can tap into this source regularly and keep you up-to-date on the increasing closeness between the Hungarian and Russian Governments. The Russians clearly want to reclaim their old Soviet Empire, maybe not with tanks this time but with the more subtle methods of subterfuge, false information and plain fear. I'm more than willing to help you. I don't need you to reimburse me. I want to keep Hungary free – over the centuries we've been ruled by the Turks, the Habsburgs, the Nazis and the Soviets. Since 1989 thanks to the USA and its NATO allies we've governed ourselves. I want to keep it that way. I want to keep the Russian Bear at bay."

Traveling on a false passport that he obtained thru his usual CIA sources, Simon arrived in the beautiful city of Budapest in time for lunch. He texted Joseph on his burner with a cryptic message 'Goulash at 1p. DH.' Joseph smiled to himself. He was looking forward to seeing DH again (DH stood for Dead Hand because of Simon's crippled left hand.) The message asked Joseph to meet Simon at their favorite Hungarian restaurant at 1.00pm in the Buda Quarter. (Budapest is a combination of the two ancient cities of Buda and Pest divided by the River Danube.) The restaurant was called Mandragora, situated off the beaten track and ideal for their meeting. Simon arrived slightly before Joseph and sat down at a table at the back of the restaurant with a full view of who was coming, going and passing by. Simon had already visited the restrooms and made sure there was still an easy exit in case of emergencies. He recognized Joseph immediately and was shocked to see how thin he had become but he still had his large, warm smile.

Speaking in German they greeted each other asking after each other's health and families. "As you can see, Simon, I'm not my usual plump self. I'm going thru several rounds of chemotherapy to cure stomach cancer. Fortunately, the doctors discovered it early enough so my chances for survival are fairly good. The only downside is that the drugs I'm having to take are not only killing the cancer cells but also killing my appetite! Please excuse me if I cannot join you in our usual goulash experience."

"No problem, my good friend. I had no idea that you were suffering so much. You didn't mention anything in your secure communications."

"I don't like to make a fuss. So what brings you to our beautiful city?"

"It's complicated so let's eat, have a glass or two of the restaurant's best Bull's Blood wine and then we can walk along the Danube and chat. Is that OK for you?"

"No problem so long as we walk slowly, I get tired quickly, you know."

"Deal."

Simon enjoyed his hearty lunch of beef goulash with Bull's Blood and was worried as he looked at Joseph picking away slowly at a beetroot salad and potatoes with mineral water. He was wondering whether it would be right to ask for Joseph's help to track down Amira – he clearly was not at all well. At the end of lunch as if he were reading Simon's mind, Joseph put down his fork and said "Simon I'm going to give you some advice. Despite the doctors' optimism I must be realistic – I won't be able to continue being your agent for much longer. The cancer will get me eventually. You need to find a replacement. I have someone in mind. You can meet her later tonight if you so wish. Her name is Erzsébet Erdész, my daughter."

"I am very sorry about your decision. I respect it and I won't try to change your mind. You've been a great friend to me all these years and you have been an outstanding colleague to work with. Why don't we take a short stroll and we can talk about Erzsébet and the reason I'm here."

"Thank you Simon. Those words mean a lot to me. By the way, I forgot to ask you about your new hand. It looks good. How does it feel?"

"It's been great. I still do the daily exercises and take the anti-rejection drugs. I get occasional spasms accompanied by some pain, it's probably the drugs I'm taking. I'll check with my doctor when I return to Paris to see if I can stop taking them. Now let's discuss Erzsébet and why she would be a good agent."

"I've invited her to dinner with us tonight if you are OK with that? All she knows is that we are friends and that you are an American diplomat. But I really want to know the reason for your visit. What brings you here? We can talk safely."

Simon told the story about the three postcards, the assault on his daughter, and the video about Ivan Ivanovich. "I think someone associated with our Embassy is working with an external party or parties, possibly Russian, to bring down my network and in the process get me fired. Our new President wants to be much closer to Russia and is causing a lot of friction at home and abroad. I know who sent these cards. I've had no contact with her for a very long time. She is Hungarian, her name is Amira Takács and she used to be an interpreter for the Hungarian Foreign Trade Department during the Communist era. I need to locate her and find out why she sent those cards. Can you help?"

"Of course I can. Her name is quite common but I have a good friend who is an expert in finding people. I will call him now while you enjoy the view of our beautiful Danube. It's always so blue."

A few minutes after Joseph called his friend, Simon's encrypted mobile rang – the display showed Philippe's name. Simon took the call "Hi Philippe, what's up?" "Papa, I've got some news about Justin. He asked me yesterday to have a drink with him. I've learnt something important. The guy who persuaded Justin to set up Suzanne is called Eric and it's the same Eric who used to work at the Embassy. Do you remember him?"

"Remember him? He used to work for me! What else did Justin say?"

"Well, he and Eric are lovers and Eric threatened that he would break up with him if he didn't do as he was told. So when Justin got hold of Suzanne supposedly for old times' sake he found out that she was flying down to Monaco, so he decided to follow her and meet up. Eric told him how to create a scene and get Suzanne arrested. He is very frightened of Eric but still loves him a lot. I promised I wouldn't tell anyone. What should I do?"

"Nothing. Say nothing to anybody. Keep it to yourself. Don't even tell your mother or Suzanne. Let me work on this confidentially so you stay in the clear. You've done a great job, Philippe. I'm proud of you."

"Thank you, Papa, au revoir."

Simon carried on looking at the Danube in the afternoon sun watching the tourists waving from the tour boats as they glided along the river. He was very worried about what his son had told him. Why would Eric want to harm his family? They got on well when they worked together; he did not agree with Eric's dismissal – he made that very clear publicly. Joseph came over and asked "Is everything OK?"

"Yes, just got some further news about the assault on Suzanne. It's becoming even more complicated but I'll get to the bottom of it. What did your friend say?"

"He'll have some news for us this evening. You can count on it."

"You know, Joseph, I don't want to tire you out so I'm going to do some sightseeing by myself for a couple of hours, revisit some old haunts that I enjoyed the last time I was here. What time do you want to meet up tonight?"

"That's very considerate of you, Simon. I'll get a taxi and we'll be at your hotel around 7p."

Simon said he looked forward to having dinner with Joseph and his daughter. He decided he would go for a long walk and made his way to Buda Castle. The Castle was originally built in 1265 by the one of the Kings of Hungary to provide protection from marauding Mongols and Tartars. Over the years it has been successively attacked, damaged, recaptured by both Muslim and Christian armies and finally was badly destroyed during WW2. It is now a massive 18th-century Neo-Baroque-style structure of more than 200 rooms. Like much of Budapest, it's a great area to explore after nightfall, when it's lit up in spectacular fashion. As Simon absorbed hundreds and hundreds of years of history, he missed the companionship of Béatrice who ordinarily would have loved to be with him. She would have wanted to discuss the beautiful paintings on display in the Hungarian National Gallery and would have delighted in seeing all the ancient artifacts in the Budapest History Museum – both places being housed in the Castle. But that was not to be – at least not until he had finished his hunt. He sent her a text on his encrypted phone – 'miss you lots. I'm in Budapest working on some leads. Love to see you when I return'. Let's hope she replies, he wished.

Feeling invigorated, Simon walked down Andrássy Avenue towards Heroes Square. It took him about two hours to reach his destination and he was constantly checking to see if he was being followed.

Partly for counter-surveillance purposes and partly to take some short rests, he stopped at Saint Stephen's Basilica and later at Liberty Square. All appeared well. No-one seemed to be checking on him. His final stop before reaching Heroes Square was the House of Terror, a museum documenting the Nazi and Soviet regimes of political repression in Hungary and a memorial to all the victims who suffered persecution, torture, imprisonment and execution. 'Unfortunately' he muttered to himself 'the current government in Hungary is just a few steps away from recreating the same atmosphere that dominated Hungarian life during the thirties thru the fifties'. He reached the famous Square that celebrates over eleven hundred years of Hungarian nationhood. Not only does it feature the seven tribal chieftains who founded Hungary but also several anti-Nazi freedom fighters from WW2 and the Tomb of the Unknown Soldier. In 1989 after the Berlin Wall fell, Heroes Square saw thousands of citizens gathered for the reburial of Prime Minister Imre Nagy who was executed by the Soviets in 1958 after the failed Hungarian Uprising of 1956. (Again another reminder for Hungarians currently living under a government that tightly controls all the major national and local media. Simon wondered how extreme would this government become in the future? How closely would it resemble past tyrannical regimes?)

Simon soon had enough of revisiting reminders of Nazi and Soviet despotism. He recalled a sonnet by the English Romantic poet Shelley who wrote these final lines in his poem –

> "Look on my works, ye Mighty, and despair!'
> Nothing beside remains. Round the decay
> Of that colossal wreck, boundless and bare
> The lone and level sands stretch far away."

The central theme reminds the reader of the inevitable decline of leaders of Empires and their pretensions to greatness and longevity.

Simon had not heard from Béatrice but he was fired up and ready to hear Joseph's news as he was waiting in the hotel lobby bar drinking a glass of cool, light white wine. He noticed Joseph arrived alone, waved him over and watched him walk slowly towards the bar. "Where's your daughter?"

"She'll here in about half an hour. I thought it better for us to talk for a while before she meets you."

"Good idea. Tell the barman what you'd like and let me have your news. I'm very eager, Joseph."

Joseph looked concerned as he spoke "My friend found Amira Takács. She is married and her last name is Ferenczy. Sound familiar?"

"It does but I can't place it."

"Well her husband is Istvan Ferenczy. He is our Minister of State Security and is related to László Ferenczy who was a notorious criminal during WW2. He was responsible for the deportation of Hungarian Jews to Auschwitz under the guidance of Adolf Eichmann. Istvan is a very powerful and dangerous man, Simon. He's responsible for carrying out our government's anti-immigration, counter-terrorism and surveillance policies. He is part Russian and is very close to the current regime in Russia, in fact very close to Ivan Ivanovich. "

"Why on earth did she marry him? I really don't care. It's just a thought. She was so anti-Russian when I knew her."

"Well perhaps you'd like to ask her! Just joking. Istvan will hang you up by your balls if he catches you!"

"Well, that may be so but I need to make contact with her somehow. I know she has a sister called Mari but I recall they lost touch when her sister moved to the USA. I think Amira said she was a bit unstable. Can your guy track the sister down?"

"I doubt it very much. That's something you'll have to do thru your CIA contacts. But I can tell you that Amira will be in Budapest tomorrow opening a new headquarters for the governing Party. It's on Rákóczi Avenue near the Novotel. You will be able to see her but security will be very tight. I recommend that you do not make any attempt to speak with her or approach her. You will be seen as a threat and could be shot."

"OK Joseph I'll follow your advice. I'll think about whether it's worth going along."

"Ah, here comes my daughter, Erzsébet. We need to change the subject quickly. Over here, Erzsébet. Come and meet my good friend Simon from America."

A tall willowy young woman walked purposefully towards their table, kissed Joseph and gave Simon a firm handshake. She sat down, smiled at Simon and asked her father what dinner plans he had made as she was very hungry. He had made none.

"Good, because I've reserved a table at the Halaszbastya Restaurant on Buda Castle Hill. Simon, you will have a wonderful view of Budapest by night. You will be amazed by how beautiful our city looks when it's fully illuminated. It's truly wonderful. Shall we go now?"

The two guys agreed, paid their bill and followed Erzsébet to the taxi that was waiting for her. 'She's certainly organized, thought Simon, and has a mind of her own.' They quickly arrived at the restaurant and were shown to their corner table. The restaurant was splendid. It had been badly damaged during WW2 and had been fully restored in the impressive style of the Habsburgs with large dining areas both internally and externally. Large Greek-style colonnades gave a regal atmosphere for dining inside while on the terrace the wide open spaces allowed diners to enjoy a breathtaking panoramic view of the Danube and the City.

As they ordered their meals, Simon noticed a rather large party of people arriving. They were making a lot of noise, laughing loudly and one of them appeared to be complaining about something. Joseph leaned across to Simon and whispered conspiratorially "If you are discrete you can see Istvan at that table over there. He has just arrived with some of his colleagues. He's the one who is making most of the noise and is wearing a blue sash. There's a problem with the table – its size or its location. I can't tell exactly but the woman next to him, I'm going to assume, is his wife Amira."

"Where are the restrooms?" asked Simon.

"Behind you. You need to go past their table. Please be careful."

Simon excused himself, got up slowly and moved away thinking 'what if she recognizes me, no problem I'll pretend I don't understand'. He decided to walk towards the terrace and returned a different way so he had an excellent view of Istvan and his spouse. 'Yes, that's definitely Amira. Wow, she has changed' he muttered to himself. She was wearing a very chic off the shoulder evening dress set off by a glittering silver necklace and a pair oval green earrings. Her hair had been coiffed in the latest Parisian style. But she had gained a lot of weight since he last saw her so many years ago! 'Eating too many noodles, too many dumplings and too much cream. Oh, I'm getting too bitchy in my middle years' he thought. Simon decided that if the opportunity arose and she left the table unescorted, he would try to talk to her. Fortunately for him, Amira did not recognize Simon and no-one at her table noticed the slender, average-looking spy walk past them.

Arriving back at his table, Simon asked Erzsébet some friendly questions about her background. "My parents died in a car accident when I was 10. Fortunately Joseph, my father's brother, and his wife took me in and eventually adopted me. I shall always be ever grateful for them doing that. I graduated from the Budapest University of Technology and Economics five years ago with a Masters in

Computer Technology and Math. I speak four languages fluently, five if you include Hungarian. Right now I work for a cyber security company in Budapest and soon I'm going to be promoted to a new role in their Artificial Intelligence team."

"Erzsébet knows what you do, Simon. She knows about our relationship plus she knows why you are here."

"Ok" Simon replied "let's finish our meal and talk some more on the terrace away from people. I can still keep my eye on Amira's table from outside."

They moved slowly to the terrace outside and spoke quietly so as not to arouse any unnecessary interest. Joseph remarked "I explained your situation to Erzsébet and your interest in the Ferenczy couple. She's ready to help you in any way she can."

"Thank you Erzsébet" Simon said with a boyish smile.

As they sat at a small table outside sipping some Hungarian liqueurs, Joseph tapped Simon's right foot and said quietly "on your right." Simon cast a quick glance and spotted Amira moving away from her table. He got up and followed her at a safe distance. She was checking her phone not looking up or around, walked past the restrooms, stopped at the entrance to the restaurant and looked around. She waved at someone, rushed down the steps and disappeared into a small opening. Simon followed her again and was delighted to see her embracing some young guy. He was built like a linebacker and was wearing a very expensive Armani suit which he filled out well. Their embrace was a passionate full-lip lock as his hands rubbed her ample buttocks and her hands massaged between his thighs. 'Not a relative I guess' Simon smiled. 'This is a gift'. Then the young man turned Amira round, grabbed her breasts and ground his groin into her rear while she moaned with undiluted pleasure. Amira was not short but this guy towered over her. Their fondling carried on for a few more minutes giving Simon ample time to shoot an HD video with his encrypted mobile phone equipped with a high-

speed 48Mp camera. He let the lovers return to the dining room
before he made any attempt to get back to Joseph and his Erzsébet.
Using his burner phone Simon tapped a quick text to Joseph saying
"All is great. Coming back in 2. DH."

Returning to the terrace sporting a wide grin he told them "we need
to leave by the rear exit as I don't want us to walk past their table
again."

Leaning against a parapet on the Széchenyi Chain Bridge, he showed
Joseph and Erzsébet the video declaring "this is gold. But I need
surveillance on them both for the next few days. Can your friend
help me, Joseph? By the way who is Amira embracing?"

Joseph replied "He looks like Istvan's head of personal security.
What's his name Erzsébet? I've forgotten."

"Karik Petrov. He's Russian. Hired by Istvan when he became
Minister. Typical Russian. Can't keep his hands off foreign women!
He was an officer in Spetsnaz. " she relayed. Simon was impressed
with her knowledge and her venom.

Joseph continued "My friend can help you again. No problem. He
can do many things, such as making annoying people disappear
forever without a trace. All it takes is cash."

"48 hour surveillance starting now. How much?"

"I'll call him. He always answers."

Joseph jabbered away in Hungarian and then said "he insists on
talking with you. His name is Mickey."

Simon took the phone and greeted Mickey. They talked in German
for a while. All Mickey wanted to know was how was he going to get
paid. Simon said he could visit him now and make an immediate
transfer into any account anywhere in the world. They agreed a price
of US$5,000.00 payable up front within the next hour. So the three

of them took a taxi to some street in the backwaters of Budapest where the dumpsters were overflowing with garbage and where there were more potholes than asphalt on the roads. Joseph asked the driver to stop at a certain address and to wait until they returned. As they exited the taxi Joseph sent a short text and Simon looked cautiously around the neighborhood checking to see if there was any one suspicious. All appeared OK. A grubby-looking door in front of them opened and a short, wiry man carrying a Glock 43 beckoned them in.

Simon asked him "Mickey?" The guy nodded and smiled showing two rows of the most even white teeth Simon had ever seen. 'Business must be good' he thought. Mickey invited them into his office which housed banks of the latest computing technology. Simon detailed the surveillance tasks that he wanted Mickey to undertake. They spoke again in German as Mickey had little English knowledge – fortunately Joseph and Erzsébet understood German very well. Then Simon completed the transfer of funds and told Mickey he would return in 48 hours.

It was clear that Joseph was feeling really tired so the taxi took him home; Simon returned to his hotel with Erzsébet as he wanted to continue discussions with her about her interest in becoming his agent after Joseph's retirement. In a secluded corner of the bar where Simon could easily see the comings and goings of all the customers, he quizzed her for over an hour about her motivation, her abilities and her contacts. He tried to trip her up by playing back to her inaccurate summaries of what she had told him – without any success! He told her about the mess he was trying to resolve in Paris. Eventually, they agreed to halt as they would be seeing each other again soon. Erzsébet returned to her apartment.

In his room Simon texted Joseph and thanked him for his help and confirmed that he was impressed with Erzsébet and would return in 2 days.

Before going to bed, Simon was so concerned about the spasms his new hand and forearm had been experiencing that he texted Guy asking him for an urgent appointment for the next day or the day after. Guy responded saying "I can see you tomorrow at 2p at the Dubois Clinic. We need to talk about Béatrice as well." Simon responded very briefly "OK" wondering what Béatrice's overly protective brother was going to say or recommend. She still had not replied to the text he had sent her from Budapest.

14 HUNT

Guy greeted Simon warmly in his examination room saying "let's take a good look at your hand and arm. Also tell me more about your symptoms." Simon explained about the spasms and the bouts of pain. He was wondering whether these symptoms were being caused by the anti-rejection drugs. After Guy had examined Simon and had asked all his questions, he took some of his blood and urine for analysis and then ordered a PET scan and an MRI. While they waited for the results they discussed Béatrice. Guy started by saying "I know you two still love each other, am I right? She tells me she still loves you."

Simon replied "I adore her and I miss her, so yes I still love her. She feels that I deceived her and I exposed her and our children to danger. I can understand her feelings. But I have a plan that I really want to share with her alone to see if I can make amends and we can return to where we left off."

Guy smiled at Simon (he rarely did this) and suggested "why don't I invite Béatrice to have dinner tonight at our apartment and you come along. I'll let her know you'll be arriving. We'll prepare a simple meal which you two can eat in a private dining room where you can talk confidentially as long as you like. My wife and I will keep out of your way until, well until you say you'd like to see us."

"Guy, that's a great suggestion. I really appreciate you doing this for us."

"No problem, Simon. I just want you and Béatrice to be back together again. Why don't you arrive at our apartment around 7.30 tonight?"

"That'll be great."

"Let's discuss the problems with your hand and forearm now."

"What do your tests tell you?"

"Well the good news is that everything looks excellent. Your blood work is normal and there's no sign of excessive residue of the meds you are taking. Your body is processing the drugs very efficiently. Your blood shows no sign of any vitamin deficiency which sometimes does cause muscle contractions. There's no sign of peripheral neuropathy of the motor nerves which control the muscles in your left arm and hand. All of the muscles and tendons look great. None of the connections I made during surgery looked stressed. You are clearly keeping up with the physical therapy I recommended. All the tests show that you are very healthy, Simon. I'm at a loss to explain why you are getting these painful episodes. Your urine sample shows that you are well hydrated. Often muscle cramps are caused by lack of fluid in the body. All I can offer as a possible diagnosis is that you are experiencing a lot of stress right now and that the weakest part of your body, your new hand and forearm, are displaying elements of this psychosomatic disorder. I'm not an expert in this field but I can recommend a good friend of mine who specializes in this area."

"I appreciate the good news, Guy. It's going to take a week or so before I have enough time to see your friend. Let me get back to you, OK?"

Guy looked slightly concerned saying "You don't want to delay it for too long as the pain might start affecting your ability to act rationally and you may not be able to sort out all these issues that are clearly causing you a lot of stress. But in the meantime my wife and I look forward to seeing you and Béatrice tonight around 7.30p?"

You'll definitely see me tonight."

Leaving Guy's clinic Simon texted Phillippe on his burner saying "I need to meet Eric tomorrow night. What's his address and phone number? Don't say a word to anyone. Love, Papa."

Simon took a taxi to the Embassy to catch up on business – he was way behind on all the tasks his department was organizing but he knew he could rely on Stephanie to pick up the slack. Unfortunately, he met Dirty Harry in one of the corridors. He was walking more slowly than usual. Simon asked "How are you today Harry?"

"Not too good Simon. It's probably something I ate that has given me this awful indigestion across my chest."

"You had better see your doctor. Don't want to take any chances do you?" Simon emphasized sympathetically.

"I just need to rest for a while. I'll be fine, you'll see. How's your new network coming along?"

"Still working on it. Back to Hungary tomorrow."

Relieved that the awkward exchange with Dirty Harry was over, Simon walked to his office and greeted Stephanie who was busy typing away at her keyboard while having a phone conversation in German. She looked different today – more attractive than usual. She was wearing a very stylish blouse with matching scarf and her hair was highlighted with light purple streaks. He waited until her phone conversation had finished and then asked "What are you working on Stephanie? Do you need any help? I'll be around for about three hours."

"Thanks but I'm good. I'm working on that Elvis Presley event at the Palace of Versailles the Ambassador is so keen on."

Simon grinned saying "I was astounded that the French permitted us to stage the event there. I couldn't believe it."

"Well you have a lot of mail to go thru, Simon. Nothing seems urgent, not like the other time, no more postcards."

"Thank goodness, that's a relief."

A new text from Philippe gave Simon the information he had asked for. Philippe wanted to know what his father was going to say and do. Simon texted back "Don't worry. I need Eric's help that's all." Simon had to think about the best way to approach Eric – knock on his apartment door unexpectedly, call him or text him? Rather than stay at the Embassy and go thru all his mail, he decided to take the Metro to Eric's neighborhood and have a look round to think thru his approach. He let Stephanie know he had to go out for a while saying "you can reach me on my mobile if anything urgent crops up. If you have time, feel free to process my mail. I can rely on you to make the right decisions."

Stephanie replied with a smile saying 'Sure, Simon, I'll take care of it for you. When will you be back?"

Simon was hurrying towards the elevator and was out of earshot so he didn't hear Stephanie's question. She continued working on the Elvis Presley event at Versailles thinking how incongruous the whole concert would appear but she would do her best as always. She didn't want to let Simon down and incur the wrath of the Ambassador.

Dirty Harry had made it clear what impression he wanted the concert to make. "Plenty of loud rock music, lots of young people clothed in tight-fitting jeans, patriotic shirts and leather gear dancing, wiggling their hips. I want a hologram of the king of rock himself playing his guitar with his famous slick hair displayed on the front entrance." She knew that the US Embassy would be a laughing stock once the concert had finished. But Dirty Harry wouldn't care – he just wanted to make sure that all the guests knew which country was #1 when it came to creating loud, unforgettable events.

Stephanie had been Simon's faithful officer since he was transferred from the UK. Born and raised in Senlis about fifty kilometers from Paris, she attended the American University of Paris where she graduated with a major in Fine Arts with a Minor in Sociocultural Anthropology. Returning to her family home, she spent two years working at the local Museum of Art and Archeology. She eventually realized that she missed the excitement of Paris and a good friend of hers let her know about an opportunity at the US Embassy. She applied for the Cultural Affairs position. Because of her language skills, knowledge of American culture acquired at University and her experience in the art world she was hired.

Because of their mutual love of art she and Simon used to spend quite a few hours of the working week talking, discussing and explaining what they individually liked. Occasionally they would visit museums near to the Embassy to see the latest exhibits. She adored the Impressionists. "To think they were ridiculed and reviled during their lifetime with some of them living in abject poverty and now their works attract long lines of tourists and connoisseurs willing to pay millions for one piece of art."

Simon replied "I hear you but unfortunately that's what happens with many new ideas and concepts. Look at the way both Copernicus and Galileo were treated when they published their findings about the Earth orbiting the Sun. Galileo was put on trial for heresy. The majority of people prefer the status quo, you know 'don't rock the boat' mentality. Then when someone comes along and says the Sun is the center of our Universe, he or she is denigrated or worse. Would you believe that in 1956 the International Flat Earth Society was founded in the UK? And it is still active now!"

Stephanie enjoyed her talks with Simon, actually she loved them. In fact she had fallen in love with him. He was the only man she felt comfortable with and enjoyed being with. He had the most boyish grin whenever he shared a joke with her about Dirty Harry's latest whims to please the White House. To spend several hours with Simon over a beautiful meal with fine wine in one of those upscale Parisian restaurants he often talked about would have been sheer bliss for her. He would share his dreams of owning works by his favorite artists – Velasquez, El Greco and Dali. How he would hang them in a secret vault on a small island and would invite his friends in to view them and relish their obvious envy. Just his very presence stimulated her, his closeness in their small office made her so happy. But she knew he was happily married and was not the slightest bit interested in a shy, rather plain work colleague who was still a virgin. She promised herself that she would keep her passion secret but rather carelessly one day she revealed her true feelings about Simon to Eric, just before he had been fired for his gay relationship. She trusted Eric much like Simon had done.

On the train Simon was thinking about Eric. During his time working at the Embassy he had been a hard-worker, a quick learner and he got on well with everyone. Simon tried to remember anything particular about Eric – his pastimes, his interests and his plans for the future. All he could recall was Eric's fascination with the ocean – he loved sailing, fishing and scuba, really anything to do with the sea. He remembered him once saying "my dream would be to get a small house on the Cote d'Azur and spend my life tanning on the beach, sailing thru the waves and writing, playing music, talking with friends on my deck".

Simon quickly found the apartment building where he lived. It was a modest block in a quiet, clean neighborhood with a few cars parked on the sidewalk to allow traffic to flow freely along the streets. Simon checked the time to see how long it was before dinner at Guy's home. He had four hours to kill. He might as well call Eric and try to see him now. This would be an entirely new experience for

Simon. He had never done 'field work' before. Most American spies worked thru third parties who carried out the dirty tasks – blackmail, pay-offs, threats and worse. It was too late to check how to do it so he threw himself into the task.

He used his burner to call Eric. Luckily, he picked up - "Who's this?" he shouted. "Hi Eric, it's Simon from the Embassy. I was hoping we could talk for a while. I was really upset that you were dismissed by the Purity Committee – I tried my best and so did the Ambassador to persuade them to let you keep your job. I have to attend my investigation in a couple of days. Are you available now to chat? I'm very close by. I can be with you in 10 minutes."

"What's there to discuss, Simon? I lost a career I loved. I won't be able to work again for the Department of State. I'm still unemployed. I will have to return to the States soon if I don't get a job with sponsorship in France. What are you proposing?"

"A way out of your current situation, that's what. Meet me outside your apartment block in 10 minutes and we can talk."

"OK, see you in ten then."

He recognized Eric as he came down the steps. He had changed a lot in just a few weeks. His clothes were shabby, his hair looked as if it hadn't been combed for days and he had lost a lot of weight. He still had the highly intelligent look in his eyes, though. They shook hands and Simon suggested they walk in the local park while they talked. "So tell me what you've been doing since you left."

"Not much. I've caught up on my reading quite a lot. Repainted some rooms in my apartment. Been spending a lot of time with Justin Heyworth, Charles' son. We walk a lot round here. This is a lovely park. How about you? Still traveling?"

"Yes, still busy as always. Trying to keep Dirty Harry happy. Let's talk about the real reason I came here to see you, Eric. I need to make an important proposal to you. I know that you persuaded Justin to set up Suzanne in Monaco but I'm not here seeking revenge. I'm looking for information. If you tell me what made you do that I am prepared to pay you a substantial amount of money – probably substantial enough to enable you to buy your dream home near the ocean may be not the Cote d'Azur but somewhere else equally enticing. I don't think for one minute you acted alone. Am I right?"

"Yes you are but what if I decline to tell you anything, what happens?"

"Then, Eric, I will go public about your affair with Justin and your complicity in the criminal provocation of my daughter. Since both Justin and Suzanne are related to senior US diplomats, the gutter Press will have a field day and your opportunities for a new career here in France or for that matter back home will be finished. I assure you I can make that happen."

"I don't doubt that you can. I have a fair idea of what your real job is at the Embassy."

"So how much would you be looking for?"

"At least US$250,000."

"That's ridiculous. I have no alternative but to contact my good friends in the Press. I will start with Der Spiegel in Germany and then move onto the Sun in the UK."

"I was only joking, OK. Make it US$100,000 and once the funds are in my bank I will tell you everything."

"So what I want from you is a typed statement revealing who asked you and why. I want names, dates, how much you were paid and what were their reasons. While you think about it I will call my bank."

Simon walked away from Eric and as he was calling his daughter in Milan his left hand started those spasms again. Fortunately, they didn't last long and there was little pain.

Suzanne was delighted to hear from her father and immediately asked what was going to happen between him and Béatrice. Simon reassured her that he was very close to resolving all the issues and he was seeing Béatrice tonight for dinner. He continued "I need your help. Do you still know my bank details from when you were paying off that loan years ago?" She did. "Well, I know you are a successful gambler and now I'd like you to place a bet on me. Can you loan me US$100,000 for a few days, no questions asked?"

"Papa, I have over US$2M sitting in my bank. Is $100K enough?"

"Wow, you have been doing well. Yes, $100K is fine. Please transfer it over the next few minutes. You will get it all back plus some extra when I've sold some of my stocks."

"There's no need to pay me more than $100K. If I'm helping you and Maman get back together, that's all I need the extra I want."

Suzanne finished the call and immediately transferred the funds to Simon's account and texted him confirmation. Simon walked back to Eric. "The funds are available. I have my laptop with me and I can pay you now. So let's go to your apartment and get working on that typed statement."

It was apparent that Eric took better care of his apartment than he did of himself but perhaps it was Justin who had made sure it was clean and smelled fresh. Simon remained standing in the lounge and asked Eric to explain the events leading up to the incident in Monaco. Eric told Simon the whole story. Following his dismissal from the Embassy, his former lover at the British Embassy told him that a very good friend of the British official (he gave her a cover name –'Rita') wanted to pay back the US Government for the way Eric had been treated. The British diplomat had been demoted not fired like Eric. Why 'Rita' was angry at the US Government wasn't clear but she paid Eric US$10,000 to create a situation which would embarrass the US Embassy in Paris.

Eric admitted that he did not want any direct involvement in any embarrassing situations that he was going to arrange; instead he seduced Justin and persuaded him to be his front man. "I remember that you and Charles were close and that your families met socially so I thought Justin could easily reintroduce himself into Suzanne's social circle and find an opportunity to carry out my plan. You may wonder why I willingly did this. I had suspected for some time that you were traveling so much for an ulterior motive. I worked out that you were carrying out some sort of espionage on behalf of the US Government since you kept having so many meetings with Walter Talbot and we all know what he is. I can't tell you how much I disapproved of your covert activities. I'm telling you, if it hadn't been for Stephanie and me, the Cultural Affairs office would have achieved nothing. You were too busy wandering around Europe. That was my motivation plus the money I was offered. By the way, Stephanie idolizes you. I bet you've never noticed have you? Anyway, I digress. When Justin told me he was going to a casino in Monaco with your daughter, I took him thru step by step on how he should get her arrested. I was very proud of my work – your daughter got plenty of negative publicity which has already reflected badly on you and the Embassy. Remember, bad news never goes away. It doesn't matter how many statements you get from the authorities saying she was innocent, people only remember she was arrested for assault in a casino and you are her father."

Simon was struggling to contain his anger as Eric pontificated and justified his actions. Determined that Eric would never get to keep the $100K, he kept reminding himself to 'keep calm and carry on' - focused on getting Eric's statement written up, recorded on video and signed by him. Simon intended using it at the Purity Committee investigation if his daughter's arrest was raised (which he felt would be the case). But he would have to get the Committee's agreement to review it in secret along with any other confidential information he obtained. During these sessions no attorneys were allowed to assist the participants; in addition the use of the Fifth Amendment had been disallowed so refusal to answer any question was treated as an act of obstruction of justice.

Eric's testimonial was completed to their mutual satisfaction and the funds were transferred to his bank account. Simon advised Eric to disappear quickly, otherwise he might be subpoenaed to appear in front of the Purity Committee. "No problem. I'll be out of here tomorrow. I rather like the idea of going to the Dubrovnik area of Croatia and enjoy the Adriatic coast and ocean. Can't say it's been a pleasure knowing you Simon. Hope I never see you again." With that Simon left and he never heard from Eric ever again.

But what Simon did not know was that before Eric left he contacted 'Rita' and told her about Stephanie's infatuation with Simon. He suggested that 'Rita' create a rumor about a mutual affair between the two of them and somehow got news of it to Béatrice. 'Rita' loved the idea, complimenting Eric on his opportunism "this rumor will help to destroy their marriage which I hear is none too stable right now. My contact in Hungary will be very pleased and I'll make sure you are rewarded again. Keep up the good work, Eric."

Needless to say Eric did not tell 'Rita' that he had just given Simon a signed confession about the assault in Monaco nor did he tell her that he was about to disappear to Dubrovnik.

Happy with the result, Simon had to rush to the Metro to be at Guy's place by 7.30p. He arrived with a few minutes to spare having rehearsed what he was going to say to Béatrice. His encrypted mobile pinged and displayed an incoming text from Joseph in Budapest. Simon was too focused on his meeting with Béatrice so he ignored the message and continued to concentrate on his dinner conversation with his spouse. Guy opened the door to his apartment and invited Simon into the lounge. He could smell the mouth-watering wafts of garlic, onions and tomatoes coming from their kitchen. "Béatrice is here and is waiting in our private dining room. We've cooked a single course meal that my wife has left for you in the room – help yourselves to as much as you'd like. Wine, cheese and fruit is on the table. We won't disturb you. Stay as long as you like."

"Thank you so much, Guy. How is Béatrice?"

"I think she's holding up well but you can see for yourself. Go straight down this short corridor and take a right into the room."

With much trepidation Simon opened the door and found his spouse sitting at the table sipping a glass of wine. "Hi Béatrice. It's good to see you. I'm so happy that you are here."

She looked up and noticed that her husband looked very careworn and seemed to have lost some weight. "You've been busy traveling again I understand. Spying or culture this time?"

"Neither. I've been trying to identify who set up Suzanne. I've found out who persuaded Justin to incite the security guard to act aggressively and I have confirmed that there is someone else behind that plot. Don't know who that person is yet but I will know very soon."

Béatrice looked interested and asked Simon without any rancor in her tone "Who persuaded Justin?"

Simon looked into his spouse's eyes thinking she looked as beautiful as the first time he saw her all those years ago at the concert in Paris when he was struck by her slim figure, her dark hair, her smiling eyes and her exceptional hands. She looked at him expecting an answer and he quickly gathered his thoughts telling her about his meeting with Eric but leaving out the bit about the $100K payment. He went on to describe his visit to Budapest reassuring her that he was very close to solving the reasons for the postcards. "As I promised you, Béatrice, I'm going to make all this pain disappear so we can return to a normal life. Once I have all the proof I need, I can attend the Purity Committee next week and clear my name and keep my job. Once I return to Paris I'm going to resign and walk away from diplomacy and intelligence gathering completely. I don't know what I want to do with my career but for sure I want to spend more time with you helping you make that important change in your music career."

Béatrice's eyes began to moisten slowly and she was about to speak but Simon interrupted her gently, saying "don't say anything yet. Let me complete my work. I will travel to Moscow after Budapest and then I have to go to the Senate hearing in DC. Just give me a week and it will all be done."

"There's just one thing, Simon that you need to know. I've just received an anonymous text from a 'friend' saying that Eric is spreading a rumor about you and Stephanie. The rumor is that you are having an affair. Is that true?"

Simon responded angrily "that's an outright lie. That rumor is all part of the plan to bring me down. You have to believe me I would never do that to you. I love and respect you too much. Eric will pay for this. To think I used to trust him implicitly. Please show me the text and I'll ask Walter if he can identify the sender."

As Béatrice handed him the phone, Simon was now even more determined that Eric would never enjoy the $100K he had given him. In fact he would disappear forever.

As he got up to leave Béatrice hugged him firmly saying "I believe you"; he kissed her tenderly on the lips and then said goodbye to Guy and his wife on his way-out. Guy turned to Béatrice and was amazed "that was short! Why was he in such a hurry? I hope it wasn't the food that made him leave so soon!"

"Don't be so silly, Guy. He's in a rush. He has to get so much done before he flies to the US for his Senate hearing."

"Well, he needs to be careful. I don't know if you are aware but his new hand is cramping and he's quite worried about it. I can't find a physical explanation for his condition. It could be caused by some type of mental stress. I've advised him to see a specialist. "

"No I didn't know. I wish you or he had told me sooner. I must leave now. Thank you so much for our dinner and getting us back together for a short time. He says he wants a complete change of career. I believe he's sincere. I really hope that all goes well for him and we can get our lives back together."

"Are you going back to live at Suzanne's while Simon is away?"

"No I shall return to our own apartment, prepare some new compositions and wait for Simon. Suzanne and Philippe will be happy to hear that their father is making such a big change in his career. They were so upset when I told them what he really did."

15 BIG REVEAL

As Simon left Guy's apartment, he remembered he hadn't read the text from Joseph. It was short and to the point. Joseph wrote that Mickey had experienced some problems with Istvan's security detail but that Simon should still come. That was all. Simon decided to change his appearance so that there was less chance of him being recognized by Hungarian officials. He had his hair dyed black with some added grey streaks, got a pair of plain contact lenses to change his eye color and bought a herringbone suit and matching tie. He wanted to look like an aging British academic. From his office safe in the Embassy he picked out a false passport and ID careful to make sure that the photos matched his new look; took plenty of Euros and US Dollars, leaving behind all his credit cards and his encrypted diplomatic phone. He would buy a new SIM for his burner phone at Charles De Gaulle airport. He had an early flight the following morning so he stayed overnight at an airport hotel – which ensured that Béatrice wouldn't have had to see his disguise during their dinner.

He went thru immigration and customs at the Budapest International Airport without any problem. He waited in the usual place for Joseph but he wasn't there. Then he spotted Erzsébet scanning the crowded airport. He walked towards her maintaining good eye contact but she did not recognize him and glanced away.

'My disguise must be working well' Simon said to himself. He went up to her and spoke quietly saying "Hi Erzsébet, it's Simon. I'm wearing a disguise."

"Oh I didn't know it was you. I spotted you but I just thought you were a stranger staring at me."

"It's me alright. Where's Joseph. I hope he's OK."

"No, he's not. He's in hospital under observation. But you can rely on me to help you."

"I'm sure I can but what has happened to Joseph? I'd like to visit him before we see Mickey."

"Later would probably be better for a visit to the hospital. He's heavily sedated and lots of family are by his bedside. I'm hoping he will pull thru, Simon. Let's grab a taxi and go see Mickey. He's expecting us."

During the short taxi ride to Mickey's office, they talked about the upcoming summit for Eastern European heads of state in Budapest that would take place in a few days. Security was on high alert because of terrorist threats so Istvan's people would be busy with that priority. Simon thought that could be both good and bad for him – good because they had something else to focus on and bad because there would be more security personnel in the field looking for suspicious behavior. As they exited the taxi Simon took Erzsébet aside and asked her what was the problem that Mickey had. "It's better for him to explain it to you. The good news is that he completed your assignment and has some really incriminating videos."

This time Mickey had his Glock 43 hidden away and he invited both of them into a comfortable conference room set up with state-of-the-art video equipment. Congratulating Simon on his excellent disguise, Mickey asked them to help themselves to coffee, tea and to a mouth-watering assortment of Hungarian pastries – nut rolls, fruit tortes and honey cakes. Simon now felt ravenous having lost his appetite over the past few days and he piled his plate high with these delicacies and filled a large mug with strong Turkish coffee. He sat at the conference table and was expecting a presentation but Mickey said "we had a problem which I believe Joseph told you about."

"I don't know the details so tell me what happened."

"During the surveillance operations on Istvan's home in Budapest, one of his more alert guys checked out our vehicle. We believe he wrote down the license plate number before we were able to escape. The plate was false, of course. But we had to get rid of the vehicle before it was found and identified. We changed the vehicle identification number and sold the car to a Romanian black marketer who has already chopped it up and is reselling the parts to Mercedes dealers in his country. I expect Istvan will be on high alert so you must be very careful when you try to contact his wife, Amira. I'm sure that once you've seen all the photos and videos we have taken you will want to "discuss" all the evidence of her affair with Karik Petrov. About the car, you know, it's amusing – it was a brand new Mercedes and it cost me US$60,000 but the Romanian paid me US$80,000 for it and will probably make $120,000 from the parts. I might get into the car parts business – buy brand new German cars, chop them up, sell the parts and double my money! OK, enough of my fun. Time to sit back and look at the evidence we found for you."

Simon sat politely saying nothing to Mickey about his story except fully expecting him to ask for some extra fee to be paid for unbudgeted expenses. He was grateful that Mickey had made a nice profit from the hassle he went thru. After this build-up Simon was ready for the show.

He would not be disappointed. Mickey's investigators had done a great job. Mickey said he would like to show them first of all one photo in particular – it was a shot of Amira talking with a woman whom Mickey didn't recognize. "Do either of you know this person?" he asked. Simon shook his head but experienced a sudden twinge in his new hand. Erzsébet shook her head as well. The photo showed Amira talking with Mary Talbot, Walter's wife.

"Ok I'll carry on with the videos" continued Mickey. It was clear that Istvan was a very serious and busy man – worked late at the office most nights, always in meetings with the Prime Minister or with his own subordinates, traveled to various districts in Hungary checking on security and visited Russia on a regular basis. He rarely took Amira with him so she was home-bound and probably bored. Consequently, she had plenty of time and opportunity to be entertained by Karik. They purposely dressed down-market and left their expensive jewelry and watches behind when they were in public - eating out at restaurants or attending sporting events - and were careful not to attract attention. But there was no way one could mistake Karik – his muscles bulged everywhere. Because Amira had gained so much weight, it was easier for her to be treated as an ordinary middle-aged Hungarian woman.

There were excellent videos of them entering Karik's home after dining out and of Amira leaving early the following morning plus excellent photos of them in restaurants holding hands, laughing and whispering to each other. All the photographic evidence was day and time stamped. On a couple of occasions the investigators had been able to bribe the Maître d' at several restaurants to confirm in writing that the couple had eaten there on a regular basis; of course the management had no idea who their guests really were as the tables had been reserved under aliases and the bills paid in cash. So Simon was very happy. Mickey's evidence together with his own smartphone video that he had transferred onto a CD would make for one 'helluva confrontation with Amira' and some clarity on the postcards.

Mickey was pleased with his work and asked Simon how many copies he wanted. Simon told him one would be OK for the moment. Turning to Erzsébet he asked "are you willing to help me plan the next step with Amira? I will have one chance to talk to her and get her cooperation. If I screw it up she will run to Istvan and I'll be toast."

Flicking her hair to one side, Erzsébet smiled and said "it would be my pleasure to help you in any way I can. When would you like to start?"

Ignoring her flirtatious gesture, Simon became all serious as he wanted no more complications in his life – he just wanted his wife back. Maybe he was misinterpreting her gesture but he was very nearly twice her age, old enough to be her father. "Let's go and see how Joseph is doing at the hospital and then we can start planning."

Erzsébet looked very perturbed and replied "OK Simon, whatever you prefer. Let's hope he's able to see visitors."

As the weather was bright and sunny, they decided to walk enabling Simon to reveal his end game to Erzsébet without anyone else hearing what was being said. "Here's what I need to achieve. I need Amira to explain in writing why she sent me those three postcards and testify that she and I do not have a child. I want to take her to the US Chargé d'Affaires at the Embassy in Budapest and he can be an unbiased third party witness to her statements. This step is very important as I doubt whether the Purity Committee in the Senate will believe me or her without his involvement. Sounds straightforward, doesn't it? But I have only one chance to get to her. That makes me very nervous. How do you think I should approach her?"

Erzsébet slowed down and smiled "I asked Mickey if he knew anything about her daily routines that take her away from her home. Like – exercising, meeting friends for coffee, dog-walking? She likes to take her dog for a short walk every morning around 10a."

"Excellent" said Simon. Erzsébet took Simon's remark as a compliment and beamed him a radiant smile.

While they worked on their plan on the way to the hospital, the Ferenczy household was becoming quite rowdy. Amira and Istvan were arguing about the security detail that was guarding her around the clock following the suspicious incident with the car outside their home. Istvan kept telling Amira "it's for your protection, my little dove. Someone is taking too much interest in us. I don't know who it is yet but I will find out, believe me. Until then I want you to have extra protection to stop anything worse happening to us. You know I love you so much and I couldn't bear it if you were hurt or kidnapped."

Amira was tired of arguing with him. She was also very worried. Perhaps he already knew about her affair with Karik and that was another reason for the 24 hour protection. Also she was starting to feel guilty about the trouble she had created for Simon. Although she still held a grudge against him for the way he left her all those years ago, he didn't deserve what he was going thru. Istvan had told her with glee about the assault on Suzanne, the rumors circulating about Simon's marriage and the expectation that the Senate would fire him. Istvan was particularly proud that his real boss in the Kremlin was showering compliments on him – compliments that would help his career.

"You can talk for a few minutes with Mister Erdész. He is still very weak though. You must take care not to tire him out" the attending nurse instructed them when they arrived at Joseph's room. Erzsébet was close to tears when she saw how weak her father was looking. He smiled slightly at them and it took all of his strength to raise one hand to say hi. There were the usual plastic tubes keeping him alive and beeping machines monitoring his vitals. Joseph tried to speak but only managed a few words "how did it go with Mickey?" Erzsébet spoke to him quietly in Hungarian letting him know that all had gone well and he was not to worry.

The nurse returned saying "it's time to go now. You can come back tomorrow if you like for a short while." As they exited Joseph's room, Erzsébet took the nurse aside and asked her what the prognosis was for her father. The nurse told her that it was not good; they would keep him pain-free for as long as he was alive but he could pass away at any time. Erzsébet thanked her for taking such good care of Joseph.

"I must come back tomorrow morning, Simon, as he may pass away soon but I don't want to let you down. I know you want to try and talk with Amira while she's walking her dog."

"Don't worry, family comes before everything. I'll take care of it. If necessary I'll ask Mickey to help me. Now you must get back home and comfort your mother."

Simon made sure that she got to the Metro station OK and then he called the US Embassy in Budapest and asked to speak with the Chargé, Andrew Weiss. Luckily, Andrew was available and Simon asked to meet him for dinner alone that night. Andrew knew Simon very well and he was more than delighted to dine with him. "By the way I received a very anxious call this morning from your Chargé, Charles Heyworth, informing me that your Ambassador suffered a severe stroke last night and unfortunately died. Frankly, he sounded very pissed that your mobile is turned off and he had no idea where you were."

"OK Andrew, I'll call Charles back right now. See you around 7p at my hotel – Zenit on Apáczai Csere János u. 7."

"You bet!"

Simon called Charles from his hotel room on his burner. Charles sounded far from calm. The tragic death of the Ambassador had shocked everyone and his widow Nancy was in a terrible state. Luckily Anna had been able to help her make arrangements to fly her and her husband's body back to the US for the funeral. "Where the f**k are you Simon? I know you are in Budapest. But what are you up to? Your phone is off. Béatrice has no way of contacting you. This is most unprofessional."

Ignoring Charles' frustration Simon asked "Are you Ambassador pro-tem now?"

"Yes, I am" he replied testily "but what has that got to do with your disappearance?"

"Nothing at all except that I'm going to tell you that you need to call Walter Talbot and ask him what I actually do."

"I know what you do" Charles responded firmly.

"No you don't. Call Walter now. Tell him you are Ambassador pro tem. He will you tell what I do. I'll be back to Paris as soon as possible."

"OK I don't understand what you're talking about but I'll call Walter. Actually I need you back tomorrow to take some of the load off my back. By the way there's talk of you being promoted to Chargé if I become Ambassador."

"Sounds good and I'll be back when I can" said Simon thinking 'those promotions will never happen' and he ended the call.

Simon took a warm relaxing shower and then proceeded to the lobby to meet Andrew. He had to think thru a new way to get to Amira now that Erzsébet would no longer be able to assist him. She would have made a good decoy.

The weather in Budapest was beginning to change – large black clouds were forming over the Danube and the winds blowing from the Hungarian plains into the city were carrying the early warnings of a cold front originating in the Russian steppes. Fat globs of welcome rain were splattering sidewalks, vehicles and unprepared pedestrians – this sudden change of weather reminded Simon of the heavy downpour that he and Amira had experienced years ago in Chamonix. 'A useful memory' thought Simon and then his attention was caught by his Montfort name being paged. Andrew had obviously asked for him at reception and since the hotel did not have a booking under Montfort they could not contact him. Simon walked quickly over where a confused-looking Andrew was waiting and, holding his elbow, Simon spoke "let's move to the bar." Andrew didn't recognize Simon but knew his voice. "Why are you wearing a disguise? Doing some covert cultural surveillance?"

Simon led him away to a quiet corner in the bar and after ordering drinks he shared with him an incomplete but truthful version of events. "So let me get this straight" Andrew summarized. "Somebody is framing you with a cock and bull story about a child you supposedly had thirty years ago with the aim of getting you fired? And you want me to be a witness to her written denial?"

"That's about it in a nutshell. I'll bring her to the Embassy tomorrow. It shouldn't take long."

"But is this legal?" Andrew asked with worry lines creasing his forehead.

"Well, I'm not kidnapping her. She'll be coming of her own free will. I'll be appealing to her better nature."

After some more Q&A between the two diplomats, Andrew agreed to help Simon. They went back a long way having joined the Foreign Service at the same time and had struck up a firm friendship which had lasted all these years. They decided to have dinner at Simon's hotel since the rain was now turning the streets into streams and the wind was howling like a wolf as it swept round the hotel corners. Not good dog-walking weather, thought Simon. Although Andrew had agreed to help Simon he couldn't quite understand the need for all the cloak and dagger intrigue that Simon was using with his disguise, false name, false ID and burner phone. Perhaps he was suffering from too much stress. He didn't probe anymore, Simon was a good friend and he was going to help him. He just hoped it all worked out well.

Back in his hotel room, Simon was still going thru in his mind how he would try to get Amira aside long enough to have a very short conversation without arousing the attention of her security guard. As he was deliberating several options, the phone in his room rang. He picked up and heard Erzsébet voice saying "how are you Simon? Did your dinner meeting go well? I have some good news – I'll be able to help you tomorrow after all."

"How come? What has happened to Joseph?

"Actually he's improved. He's sitting up and talking and what's better he's eating. I have just come from the hospital. Now that he's a bit stronger he's going to have a series of more tests tomorrow morning. So I can help you, you see."

"That's great news. I was actually finalizing in my mind what I was going to do tomorrow. And now with your help it's much clearer. Can you come to my hotel around 7a for an early breakfast and we can go thru it all? By the way, your role entails you looking and acting seductively. OK?"

"Sure, no problem. I can come now if you like. I'm free. We'll have plenty of time to go thru your plan in fine detail."

"That's very thoughtful of you, Erzsébet, but I need to catch up on a lot of Embassy work and then get a good night's sleep."

"OK Simon, I understand. I'll see you at 7a for breakfast. Sleep well."

Before he tried to go to sleep (his mind was whirring thru all the possibilities of what might go wrong the following morning and how he would recover the situation) he set aside two photos to give Amira. One shot featured Amira laughing during the big thunderstorm in Chamonix years ago. On the back he wrote the words spoken by a stranger 'il pleut comme une vache qui pisse'. He signed that photo simply 'Simon' and hoped it would prove that he was Simon Montfort not some weirdo in the park. The other photo was a shot of Amira and Karik, both naked, making out on a balcony of a hotel in Lake Balaton. Simon wrote a short note on the back using her pet name only they knew -

'Mia, you need to call me on this number within one hour otherwise your affair with Karik will be published all over the European Press. Your life and Istvan's will be changed forever. Simon.'

He sent a quick text to Béatrice reassuring her that everything was going to plan and sending her his undying love.

The upcoming confrontation with Amira together with the raucous noise of some celebration that went on until the early hours kept Simon awake and alert for a good part of the night. He didn't complain about the revelers because he didn't want to attract any attention to himself. He had eventually fallen asleep and swore at the alarm that woke him early at 6a reminding him to do some physical therapy before breakfast.

The awful storm had passed and sunlight was quickly drying out the busy streets of Budapest as he went downstairs to the restaurant to meet Erzsébet. She was dressed to seduce, as he had recommended. Her long hair had been styled into a low twisted bun displaying her curvaceous neck; the low décolletage of her summer dress accentuated her toned upper body and the knee line showed off her shapely calves. "You certainly look the part" Simon complimented. Pretending not to understand Erzsébet asked "what part Simon?"

Simon looked at her pensively saying "Really? OK, you look ready to distract Istvan's whole security detail. Is that better?"

"Yes much. Why don't we have breakfast? There's a table in the corner over there, I know you like to sit in corners."

Simon went thru his plan to confront Amira. "She lives with her husband in a gated community near Orczy Park. Luckily, there is only one entrance/exit so we won't miss her or her security. We'll get there early. The sunny weather will hold so I expect she'll be taking her dog for the daily walk. On my sign your job is to engage the security guard in conversation – ask him for a light, the time, directions – anything really to keep his eyes on you and off Amira for 30 seconds. That's all the time I'll need to tell her what to do. I will have left a small envelope with two photos and some directions for her to pick up. I will trigger a preset signal to your mobile that will set off a brief alarm – that will be your sign to finish your conversation with the guard and meet me at the nearest Metro station, Nagyvarad Square. After she has picked up the envelope and followed my instructions, she will call me within the hour. Mickey has a limo ready to take her and me to the US Embassy where she'll make a statement. I don't want her to know about you. I don't want you to be overtly involved if anything goes wrong. Also I don't want her to be spooked by the presence of a stranger."

They arrived at Orczy Park around 9.30a giving them time to reconnoiter before Amira arrived. The park smelt fresh and inviting after the previous night's torrential rain; there was an impressive range of different types of trees to sit under including chestnuts, poplars, black poplars, willows, lindens and yews. They chose a small secluded bench not far from the entrance where they could easily see who was coming but shady enough to give them enough cover. They rehearsed the plan one final time and then Simon removed the envelope from his jacket balancing it on top of a trash can next to him. Erzsébet recommended she should walk away from Simon and move closer to the entrance. Simon agreed and within a few minutes he spotted Amira with her small dog coming into the park. Seconds later she was followed by a young-looking guy in a black suit and stylish sunglasses with a bulge under his left arm. Fortunately, he walked with a bored or tired look on his face and he slouched like a lout that stands at street corners. Simon signaled Erzsébet who came up behind the young guy saying "pardon me sir but I'm lost. Can you tell me the way to the lake? There are no signs and I have no map." The lout turned round with a look full of disdain to face the voice, ready with an unfriendly response but stopped himself short when he saw Erzsébet's sheer youth and beauty. Instead he smiled lasciviously displaying an uneven row of irregular, stained teeth and could hardly put two words together, he had been struck dumb. He managed to eke out a few words and kept staring at Erzsébet while Simon was bending down as if to speak to Amira's dog but saying to her "I'm Simon. I know about your affair with Karik. Say nothing otherwise you will be finished. There is an envelope behind me. Pick it up. Read the contents and call me within one hour. If you don't, you and Karik will feel the full force of Istvan's wrath." With that he got up, sent the signal to Erzsébet and walked quickly to the Metro station. Erzsébet politely disengaged herself from her conversation with the guard saying she had received an urgent text from her mother to return home at once.

The guard watched her walk away with a bemused look on his face and then with a big yawn remembered what he was supposed to be doing. He went over to Amira who was examining something and asked if everything was OK.

Amira was in a state of shock but she daren't show it to the guard. She had seen him gawping at some young woman's backside disappearing in the distance after she had picked up Simon's package and just assumed he was being horny.

"There's no problem. I'm going back home. You look tired. Why don't you get a few hours' sleep and then you'll be fresh for your next shift. I'll clear it with your boss, Karik." Making sure that he was on his way, Amira read thru Simon's message again and had another look at the photos. She was devastated. How did he find out? Should she call Karik and get his advice? He probably would want to blow Simon's head off. That was one option for sure. No good calling Istvan. That would be tantamount to suicide. She decided to call Simon and see what he had to say.

Simon's phone rang as he and Erzsébet were standing outside the entrance to Nagyvarad Square Metro station. "Hi who is this?" hissed Simon.

"It's Amira. I'm following your instructions. What do you want from me?"

"We need to meet. Come to the south entrance of Nagyvarad Square Metro station. Be there in 15 minutes. If I see any of Karik's or Istvan's goons I'll go straight to the European Press that will love to publish my story. Understand?"

She mumbled her agreement.

Simon turned to Erzsébet and asked her one more favor. "I've asked Amira to come to this entrance. I'd like you to be at the north entrance and if you see any sort of police or heavies or goons, call me immediately and I'll leave. After 15 minutes you go home. Wait for my call later today. I could not have done this without your help, Erzsébet. I will always be indebted to you." He hugged her and said "talk to you later." She smiled and left him waiting apprehensively. He called Mickey and asked him to send a limo to the station.

A very distraught Amira walked slowly to the Metro station, not sure what to expect and equally importantly not sure how to behave. She had a wonderful life style with Istvan – influence, prestige, wealth, three beautiful homes, a faithful and diligent husband but she was bored. That was the prime reason for her affair with Karik. He was a big, strong man of action; he was exciting and resourceful. But she wasn't prepared to lose her position because of some side show with a Russian former special ops warrior. So, she would be contrite and humble, maybe cry a lot at the right time because the Simon she remembered could be easily manipulated.

She walked up to the south entrance of the Metro station but could not spot Simon. She called his burner but it went to voicemail. She was confused – perhaps he had changed his mind, perhaps Karik had been told by her guard about the incident in the park and somehow had arrested Simon, perhaps and so on.... As she was daydreaming, a black Mercedes with blacked-out windows came round a nearby corner very quietly and parked right opposite her. Simon opened a rear door, got out quickly and escorted her into the limo.

"Where are we going?"

"Somewhere very secluded so we can have a long talk" Simon told her. "It's best for you to say nothing until we arrive. Give me your mobile phone."

It was a short 11 minute drive to the American Embassy. As they drove Simon turned off her mobile, destroyed the SIM card throwing the pieces thru the car window. He then ground her phone underfoot and asked the driver to dispose of the pieces at Mickey's office.

They were expected by Embassy Security. Simon displayed his diplomatic pass and a visitor pass for Amira; they were quickly shown into Andrew's office. Simon greeted Andrew and introduced Amira. Andrew assured them that his office was not bugged and there were no recording devices. He said they could stay there as long as Simon liked.

Amira was getting very worried. She was on American territory unable to contact anyone for assistance from her government. "What's going to happen to me?" she asked as Andrew left his office.

"Nothing if you cooperate" replied Simon brusquely.

She then started crying. Simon passed her some Kleenex and waited impatiently until she had finished. "I don't have all day for this, Amira, and I'm sure you don't. Let me outline what I need you to do and as long as you comply you can go home to Istvan safe and sound."

"So what do you want?" she growled.

"A full signed confession, that's what I want" was Simon's simple reply.

He told her what he knew – Eric's attempt to frame Suzanne, her attempts to incriminate Simon, her affair with Karik and her sister Mary's involvement in the plot to destroy his career and network. He showed her more photos and videos proving her infidelity. What he didn't know were the reasons why she had agreed to bring Simon down. Amira decided not to fight Simon nor to play the innocent, contrite little woman and agreed to fill in the gaps of his knowledge and agreed to being recorded.

"You asked me for the reasons why I wanted to bring you down. Believe me, I did not want to but a senior official in the Kremlin told Istvan it would be in his long term career interests to carry out the President's plan. The Kremlin know I have a sister in the USA who is married to the CIA Head of Station in Paris. I was persuaded to reconnect with her and offer her a large cash incentive to help me. It wasn't difficult because her friend in the British Embassy had just been demoted for his gay affair with Eric; she was upset that Eric had been punished by the Americans and more than anything else she was fed up with the constant compliments that her husband Walter paid you. Mary wanted to get back at the diplomatic service and unfortunately she agreed to target you. The rest you know except for one fact – I believe there's someone else who is working for the Kremlin. I don't know who this person is or where they are based. My sister is saying nothing apart from dropping hints."

Simon pondered for a moment thinking he needed to tread carefully. Clearly, Walter's spouse Mary was part of the plot along with Eric, Amira and Istvan. How many others were there he didn't know about? He would have to find out very quickly as otherwise his whole plan for a wealthy retirement with Béatrice would be at risk.

Once Simon had transcribed her confession and corroborative statements, he asked her to read thru her whole statement before

Andrew returned to witness all the written, audio and video testimony. With that done, Simon and Amira returned to the same Metro station in Mickey's limo. Keen to see no more of her he spoke a last few cold words "Amira, I hope I hear nothing more from you directly or indirectly."

"I'm sorry, Simon. I know you don't believe me. I didn't mean to hurt you and your family. I was forced to do this." She exited the limo, took one last look at Simon thinking how much he had changed since the blissful days in Chamonix. She walked slowly back home thru the same park not sure what to expect when she reached her beautiful apartment.

Simon texted Erzsébet that everything had gone well and he was on his way to visit Joseph. She texted back saying she would see him there. On the train feeling somewhat relieved that he was carrying Amira's confession but at the same time feeling concerned about her revelation of a yet another player, he texted Béatrice to reassure her that he was well and was going to Moscow. She replied immediately saying "Take care, love you so much". He arrived at the hospital and was happy to see Joseph walking slowly along the corridor unaided. "Great to see you on your feet again, my friend."

"Tomorrow I shall be running around Orczy Park" he replied jovially.

"That reminds me, I have to say what a great help Erzsébet was this morning. She will make a great agent when you decide to retire. Give her my warmest regards when you see her. Regrettably, I'm in a hurry, I must get ready to travel to Moscow. I have to say goodbye for now." With a warm handshake he left Joseph in the corridor knowing that he would probably never see him or Erzsébet again.

Simon checked out of his hotel and arranged for Mickey to take him back to his office where he changed his disguise and documents plus picked up another burner. He thanked Mickey for all his help, paid him handsomely and arrived at the airport in time for his flight to

Moscow. Once in Russia's capital, he would have one last favor to ask of Alexei, in fact two last favors. As he waited to board the flight he texted Alexei letting him know he was coming and he would be in touch as soon as he landed.

16 ALEXEI

It takes a little over 2½ hours to reach Moscow by plane from Budapest. The airport was bustling; people were yelling to one another to hurry up, to get out of the way, get their documents ready for inspection and so on. Simon realized it was Shrovetide. Banned under Communist rule, the Christian celebration of penance and confession now consists of several days of festivals, fairs and carnivals honoring this religious period. Thousands of Russians travel across the country carrying special foods and gifts for families and friends creating havoc for the overworked and underpaid security and immigration staff at airports. Many officials were just waving people thru after a cursory check on their papers and declarations; Simon was using a false Russian passport and ID but spoke the language fluently with a good Muscovite accent. An official stopped him and asked where he had come from "I was attending a conference in Budapest on statistical thermodynamics" (there was such a conference while he was there). The official looked blank and waved him thru.

On leaving the terminal he noticed that the taxi line looked over a mile long so he took the less crowded train and Metro to the center of Moscow. One enduring aspect about Communism that Simon admired was their adherence to a policy of clean and inexpensive public transport. Not so nowadays, he quickly saw as he entered the car. Cigarette butts, used syringes and discarded food littered the floor and aging seats. The stench of second-hand, stale smoke from Belomorkanal cigarettes combined with the sickly odor of cheap Maroussia perfume made him get off at the next station and grab a very expensive taxi to finish his ride to the center of Moscow. He texted Alexei confirming his arrival and asked to meet him at a prearranged location near Simon's modest hotel. Alexei confirmed he would be there at 5p.

The driver insisted on being paid in Euro or US$ bills as the ruble's value was falling daily causing rampant inflation. They agreed an amount, still too high in Simon's opinion but he didn't want the driver to complain and call the Moscow police. The hotel was modest (a nice way of saying down-market) but located close to Neglinnaya Street, the home of the Central Bank of the Russian Federation. The hotel clerk took Simon's passport looking at it briefly before returning it (foreign passports are copied and recorded for the local police.) He took an elevator to his room which was sparsely furnished but clean – 'this is OK as I'm here for two nights max.' He showered and changed for his meeting with Alexei wondering whether he would still be accommodating like last time but Simon was willing to give him some financial incentive this time. They met at a nearby Georgian restaurant named Café Khinkalnaya. Alexei was born in Georgia when it was part of the Soviet Union and he loved their cuisine – Simon remembered he loved hot dishes like chopped veal and pork with rice, stuffed in vine leaves or fried chicken in cream sauce with garlic as they reminded him of his mother's cooking when he was a child in Tbilisi.

Simon wandered around the outside of the local buildings appearing to enjoy the architecture but waiting until he saw Alexei's bulky figure coming towards the Café. Alexei spotted Simon without recognizing him until Simon spoke and then gave him a warm bear hug of a greeting planting kisses on both of Simon's cheeks. "I know you want something from me, Simon, but all the same I am so happy to see you and I want to tell you the good news about my daughter."

Over their meal of hot, spicy Georgian specialties accompanied by several glasses of robust Saperavi red wine from the Kakheti region they updated each other about their families and careers. Simon avoided the issue of Amira but did speak at length about Eric because that's where he needed Alexei's help. Alexei had double good news; his daughter was totally clear of the disease and was back home in Moscow living independently and holding down a career in finance; Alexei had been promoted to the position of President of the Central Bank, appointed by Ivan Ivanovich himself. Simon congratulated him heartily and was pleased that his relationship with Ivan would now be much closer and he would be less critical of him. But within a few minutes Simon's anxieties increased as Alexei started berating Ivan for his hypocrisy and his preference for playing spies' rather than concentrating on the grave economic and health issues that Russia faces.

"You know, Simon, that Aids and Alcoholism are the two main causes of our problems today and Ivan Ivanovich refuses to even listen to any sane recommendations to treat or help our citizens." Simon looked concerned as Alexei spoke. "Don't worry, I can speak like this here in this restaurant because all the staff and most of the guests are Georgians. And as you know, relations between Russia and Georgia have always been complicated."

Over glasses of strong local pomace brandy and cups of dark, rich Georgian coffee Alexei asked Simon "what really brings here, Simon?"

"I'll tell you but is there a small, private room we can go to?"

"No problem. I'm sure the owner will let us use one of small private dining rooms."

The owner, Grigol, a large man with a wide, friendly smile and a huge black mustache led them into a room two levels above the main restaurant and said to Alexei in Georgian *"veravin gaanadgurebs ak"* *no-one will disturb you here.* He then invited them to choose any table and left an unopened bottle of brandy for them to enjoy.

"He is giving us this fresh bottle as his present so we have to drink it all otherwise we have to pay for it if we don't" Alexei explained with a twinkle in his eye.

"We had better start then" replied Simon busily opening the brandy.

After several toasts Simon told Alexei the whole story about his former assistant, Eric Haupt. He ended by saying "within the next seven days I need Eric to be gone for good and I also need his bank account scrubbed so there's no record of any transactions with me. He has moved from Paris to the Croatian coast near Dubrovnik. He loves the ocean – swimming, snorkeling, kayaking, etc. He will be very easy to trace. His death needs to look like suicide – perhaps drowning. After your guys have disposed of him we can share however much of the US$100,000 I paid him is left. I'll give you the details of my off-shore bank account in Cyprus. After that is done, scrub his account for me. Any questions, Alexei?"

"Not at all. Very straightforward."

"Good. I promise you this request will be the last time I will ask you for any more favors. You will not hear from me again. Just confirm to me when you have completed the assignments."

"Why won't I hear from you anymore? What will you be doing?"

"Can't tell you much because I don't really know. I have an important meeting next week in Washington at a Senate hearing. This will be a big deal. Whatever the result, I will be doing something completely different and leaving the life of deception, blackmail and murder behind."

"Well, Simon, I will always be in your debt because without the help of your brother, you and Dr. Biche my dear daughter would be dead by now. Whatever you do, I sincerely hope that you and your lovely wife Béatrice can still meet up with my wife and me somewhere in the world before we are all too old to travel. Let's finish this bottle and you can get back to your hotel." The two guys embraced for the last time and went their separate ways.

In his room despite the fact his head was swimming from too much brandy he texted Béatrice saying he was returning home the next day.

The phone in Simon's room rang as he was getting ready to go to sleep. A male Russian voice spoke quietly to him "Simon Montfort, I have a car waiting for you. The meeting you requested will take place tonight. You have 15 minutes to get down here. Is that a problem?"

Fully expecting this call but not as late as midnight, Simon replied "No. I'll see you outside the hotel."

The following day as Simon traveled back to Paris, Alexei began to work on the elimination of Eric Haupt. He knew no-one in Croatia who could provide the kind of expertise he needed so he contacted an old colleague of his in Serbian Intelligence explaining that he had 'a small job for two ex-military guys who would ask no questions about making a young American in Dubrovnik disappear for good'. (Serbia and Russia had many cultural, language and religious ties plus their intelligence services had cooperated on many projects in the past).

He went on "I don't want to have any contact with these guys, I want all communications to go thru you. I will pay you and them very generously."

His old colleague replied "you can't leave the old career alone can you, Alexei? Anyway it will cost you around US$30K. That includes my fee and all expenses. To be paid into my Swiss account."

"Agreed" was Alexei's immediate reply. "Tell me about them. No names, though."

"Two guys spring to mind. We've used them several times in the past in Kosovo to assassinate local politicians and carry out car bombings to stop the Kosovars seeking independence from Serbia. They recently became members of the new Serbian police force in Kosovo so they are in a good position to create unrest should we decide it's in Serbia's interest to have another civil war down there. Anyway, they are very reliable and physically very capable of carrying out any operation. They know Croatia well, speak the language fluently and they can get in and get out undetected. Interested?"

"Yes, very" replied Alexei with a big smile. "My client wants the elimination to look like an accidental drowning. Any problem?"

"None at all. In fact, they would love that. Both of them are strong swimmers and have done this type of operation in the past. All they'd need from you are some photos of the target and his name or alias he'll be using."

Alexei confirmed he would send that information by encrypted email. He let his contact know that Eric was gay.

Being somewhat complacent, Eric had used his current American passport to catch a flight to Dubrovnik. Once there he had rented a small apartment in his own name and had used his own credit card to buy some swimming and diving gear. He was so relieved to have left all his problems behind in Paris and so elated to get the better of Simon, he had not planned his escape thoroughly. Sitting on the apartment's sun deck with a glass of chilled local Antunovic Grasevina white wine, he was riveted by the splendid view of Lokrum Island's nudist beach. It was situated about 2,000 feet from his apartment and he was straining to get some sexy photos of the many healthy, athletic men cavorting along the beach or diving from the rocks into the Adriatic.

He promised himself 'tomorrow I'm going to treat myself to a boat excursion over there and then hang around all day getting some sun in the hopes I can pick up some guy or even guys for a romp later.' Little did he know that he would be meeting two guys the next day but not for a romp....

As Eric was getting his kick taking photos of the nudist beach, the two killers had crossed the Serbian/Croatian border near the town of Apatin, Serbia with no difficulty. They made their way by bus and train overnight to Zagreb and then took another train directly to Dubrovnik. They paid cash for everything and in case they were questioned by the local police they carried excellent counterfeit Croatian ID's. Arriving in the late afternoon, they checked into a tourist hostel and changed into beach clothing to begin their search for Eric. He was easy to find.

They stopped at the Dubrovnik tourist information office and, explaining that they were kayaking guides, they had mislaid the address where their American client Eric Haupt was staying. They were talking with a young, attractive receptionist and asked "Can you help us please? We are supposed to meet him this afternoon. We have just started our business and it's so embarrassing to not know where we can find him."

The young receptionist was new to her job and, impressed by their suntanned muscular physiques, she shyly searched the office records and finally said "I've found him. I'll write down his address. He only arrived yesterday and I'm surprised he's had time to book a kayaking trip."

Ignoring her insinuation, one of the killers smiled boyishly at her and said quietly "you've been most helpful. Perhaps we can repay your kindness tomorrow by buying you lunch at the Vapor Restaurant. Is 12noon good for you? My name is 'Josip' and my friend is 'Marko'."

Vapor, situated in the Hotel Bellevue, overlooks the Adriatic and is known for its high-end, original cuisine. 'Josip' was betting that the receptionist would never had eaten there but would know about the restaurant's excellent reputation.

Flattered by the attention that 'Josip' was paying her, she replied "my name is Lucija. I'd like to bring my friend Marina with me, she's over there." 'Marko' looked in the direction Lucija was pointing and saw a rather plain, older woman talking with a tourist. He turned and putting on his best smile said "Sure, why not? We'll enjoy seeing you both tomorrow."

Once outside the tourist office, Josip snarled to his colleague saying "I wouldn't mind seeing Lucija again but Marina doesn't look your type, eh 'Marko'? Let's find this MF and finish the job."

Marko grunted a reply "first we'll go to his apartment and see if there's any sign of him there. If not, I reckon he'll be on Lokrum Island like most tourists when they first arrive here."

They found a good vantage point where they could observe Eric's small apartment without arousing any curiosity. After an hour or so of observation, they concluded he wasn't there and they hired a two-seater kayak to take them swiftly over to Lokrum.

On Lokrum, Eric was sunbathing surrounded by many fine examples of both male and female European nudity. The killers were rowing quickly round the island and after a few minutes noticed Eric's white body soaking up the sun. He had attempted to strike up a conversation with several guys but no-one wanted to do more than pass the time of day with him. 'Not much of a pick-up place' he muttered to himself. Then he noticed two muscular guys getting out of a kayak. 'I'll try once more and see if either or both of these guys are interested'.

Well, they both were but not for the reasons Eric was harboring. Eric nodded diffidently in their direction and they both smiled in response. Coming over closer to him, they introduced themselves as 'Blago' and 'Toma' and explained they were on a short kayaking vacation. He was excited to be with such delightful specimens of the male physique; they both spoke English very well and each had a very seductive sense of humor. The three of them talked about swimming, diving and kayaking for a few minutes until 'Blago' asked "would you like to come with us on a short kayaking trip today at sunset? We'll take you to some really beautiful caves further along the coast. The views at that time of day are out of this world. If you want we can take you into one cave in particular where there's a waterfall and if you look up you'll see the sun shedding its last rays of the day thru an aperture formed by the winds high up in the rock."

"Sounds wonderful" exclaimed Eric. He could hardly believe his luck. 'Toma' said "meet us over there on that small beach one hour before sunset. We'll have a spare kayak for you to borrow. 'Blago' will bring some wine and we can all have some fun later on." Eric returned to his apartment imaging what would happen with these two exciting guys.

Later the killers arrived on the secluded beach, making sure they were there before Eric. They still had the two-seater kayak they had rented that day and a spare which they had stolen an hour ago from a sleeping tourist. They rehearsed the operation to kill Eric one more time and felt confident that all would go smoothly. 'Toma' spotted Eric first walking towards them carrying two bottles of wine. He was dressed in a pair of tight yellow swim shorts and a multi-colored tank top that was too small for him. 'Toma' whispered to 'Blago' – "he's not exactly dressed to kill is he? He deserves to be put down just for wearing such a ridiculous outfit." 'Blago' laughed saying "your sense of humor will be the death of you, Toma."

Eric walked up to the killers holding both arms outstretched offering them the bottles. 'Toma' thanked Eric and asked him if he would like to share the twin kayak with 'Blago'.

"That would be nice" replied Eric "you are so thoughtful". He couldn't keep his eyes off their tight swim shorts and their trim waists, wondering how big and powerful their manliness would be when he took their shorts off. 'What a night we'll have' he thought.

The killers' plan was to tire Eric out with a lot of rowing and get him tipsy with the wine so by the time they reached the remote cave he would be totally helpless. After 30 or so minutes Eric complained "Ooh guys, all this rowing is making me tired and thirsty! I need to take a rest and have some wine."

"Sure, drink as much as you like. There's plenty." said 'Blago'. "We need to keep going otherwise we'll miss seeing the sun thru the aperture."

After around an hour of rowing and drinking, Eric was wasted. They had entered the cave and 'Toma' said they could take it easy now and suggested they went for a swim. They gently helped Eric out of the kayak and took off his clothes. Expecting a sensuous and exciting romp in the water, Eric was surprised when 'Toma' dived down and took hold of his feet and 'Blago' put his strong hands firmly on his shoulders and pushed him down. They tortured poor Eric. They played with him like a cat would with its prey. They would let him come up and tell him to take a deep breath and before he had fully inhaled they would push him down again. And so it went on. Eric surfaced at least five times, each time spluttering and coughing. Looking at 'Blago' with panic-stricken eyes, he screamed "please, please stop! Why are doing this to me? "

"Because we are being paid a lot of money to kill you, Eric" laughed 'Blago' cruelly. "It's now time for you to say goodbye" added 'Toma' still holding onto Eric's limp feet as he rose up briefly.

They both hung onto Eric as he struggled for the last time against the weight of the Adriatic salt water gushing into his gaping mouth and then flow painfully into his laboring lungs. After less than a minute, he went limp and made no sound or movement. Making sure he was dead, they wedged his lifeless, naked corpse between some rocks in the cave. They then destroyed the kayak they had stolen.

Pleased with their work and telling each other how much they had enjoyed the experience, they returned to their tourist hostel. After a quick change of clothes, they went to a local bar to celebrate. They decided against staying one more night and have lunch with Lucija and Marina from the tourist information office the following day. As luck would have it, they spotted the two women in the bar and went over to explain they had to leave early in the morning "why don't we go out tonight and have some fun?" asked 'Josip'. They all went bar-hopping and eventually ended up at Lucija's apartment after midnight. After a bout of noisy sex which left the two women disappointed and feeling defiled, the killers quickly departed and disappeared back to Serbia.

Some weeks later a lone kayaker came across Eric's body floating in the cave. His bloated and grey corpse was filled with gas, his eyes had popped out and his tongue was protruding grossly out of his mouth. His whole body was covered with small cuts where fish and other sea creatures had been feeding. The rocks had also grazed his body as the powerful waves threw it against the inside of the cave. Understandably, the kayaker was very unwell but managed to make a full report to the authorities.

The two killers returned to Belgrade and made their full report to the Serbian officer who had hired them. They showed him evidence of Eric's corpse and he handed over their full payment in cash. We don't know what they did or where they went after that short meeting – all we do know is that some days later two dead bodies were found floating in the Danube. Their eyes had been removed; no identification or any documents or cash were found. The Belgrade authorities were able to identify them from their fingerprints as members of a Serbian paramilitary group. Their names were not made public. The media ran a short article about their deaths, blaming Kosovo Moslems for the atrocities.

17 PREPARING FOR THE PURITY COMMITTEE

At the same time that the killers were carrying out their mission in Croatia, Senator Pius from Mississippi was leaning back in his elegant chair with a long tally pole in his hands. Like a gunfighter in a Western movie would cut a notch in his firearm to record each of his kills so the Senator was cutting two more notches in the tally pole after yesterday's hearings when two Federal employees were found guilty of sinful transgressions. These two unfortunates like many more preceding them had lost their livelihoods and their social standing. He carefully put the pole back along with all his other tally poles into a hidden closet in his office saying "two more delinquents bite the dust."

In fact so many Federal and State workers were being fired every day that it was causing the whole system of government to suffer from bouts of constipation. There was a serious lack of personnel who could be promoted or hired and trained to fill the ever increasing number of open positions. Decisions had to be deferred, meetings canceled, implementation of legislation delayed and courts closed down because the apparatus of the bureaucracy was bunged up. Citizens were complaining to Congressmen and Senators; the media was all over the issue publishing harrowing stories of neglected and abused children due to lack of case workers; school closures caused by insufficient teachers; airports operating on four day weeks because of too few security officials. But the white-haired, wily Senator from Mississippi and his two male colleagues from the Bible-belt stuck to their guns. With AR15's in their left hands and Bibles in their right hands they stood on the steps of the Senate assuring the cheering crowds that "we shall continue to carry out God's Work until we have drained the national swamp of immorality, adultery and corruption. We'll do it State by State no matter the cost to us in the short term."

 Senator Pius's two colleagues (both from neighboring States) escorted him down the steps to his black Suburban complete with a Secret Service detail, shook hands with him and watched him drive off to his apartment in DC where he would carefully go thru the detailed reports that had been compiled by his investigative staff for next week's hearings including Simon's.

Simon was watching the smiling trio of senators on his TV at his home in Paris. He was happy to be back relaxing in his favorite comfy chair. He had left Moscow without any fuss and had managed to remove some of his disguise in the First Class bathroom aboard the flight. No-one noticed, they were too busy with their electronic devices or they were sleeping off the effects of the free booze. He had torn up his fake Russian passport and ID into very small pieces and, wearing disposable gloves, mixed them up with the used paper towels in the trash. At the CDG Airport in Paris he made a trip to the restroom before entering Immigration and Customs so he could alter his disguise to match his diplomatic passport. He knew that security cameras monitored the entrances and exits to all restrooms scanning for suspicious travelers so they could be 'flagged' for interrogation. But Simon also knew that the 'flagging' computers used an Artificial Intelligence program with very limited capabilities. He felt safe as he exited the restroom looking like Simon Montfort the diplomat and breezed thru the all the security checks with a broad smile waving his diplomatic passport.

He switched off the TV and jumped up sprightly when he heard

Béatrice entering thru the front door calling his name. They embraced for a long time and simultaneously asked each other how they were. They laughed and Simon asked his wife to go first. "Everything is good now that you are back. I've missed you so much – missed you in our bed, missed you when I'm with our children, missed you when I need to talk about my new career – I could on forever."

Simon poured them two glasses of chilled Sancerre white wine from the Loire Valley. They sat side by side on their loveseat and gently clinking his glass against hers Simon said "here's to our reunion and a new start for both of us. Let's move on from the despair of the past few weeks and look forward to new adventures in our lives."

Holding Simon's right hand Béatrice told him about her meetings with conductors and music producers discussing her plans to become a full-time composer/arranger; she explained to them the reasons why she could no longer play in an orchestra -because of her increasing deafness. They had sympathized with her and had promised to help her as much as they could. "But they all told me that I would have to go back to school and learn about editing software, digital workstations and sound mixing. With those skills under my belt together with my orchestral experience and a degree in music I should be ready to go out and network, network, network and finally network until I get some projects."

Her humorous exaggeration made Simon laugh. "That's great, you'll enjoy learning new skills. You are a quick study plus you are a natural networker, you'll be successful and I would love to help you" Simon said encouragingly.

They decided to go out for a quiet, romantic dinner and went back to a small out-of-way bistro they used to visit when they were much younger. It was still in business although under new ownership and the food was as good as ever. Small round tables covered in immaculately white linen had been set up outside, along the

191

sidewalk. A striped canopy perched overhead to catch the rain or anything else that might spoil the food and atmosphere. Plenty of couples and small groups of customers of varying ages were eating, drinking and conversing leisurely over their dinners. Seated in close proximity to another couple they spoke quietly about their children and their careers. As the bistro became less busy Béatrice asked him "so what happened in Hungary and Russia?" Simon quietly shared with her most of what had transpired. He omitted the treachery of Walter's wife, Mary, and Amira's remarks that 'there's someone else who is working for the Kremlin'. He was in a quandary about whether and what he should tell Walter before he revealed it to the Purity Committee. He would have appreciated Béatrice's perspective but he thought it more prudent to hold back. And anyway Amira might have been trying to make out that she knew more than she really did – only he and one other person knew the whole truth. His late night meeting in Moscow before his departure for Paris had gone very well – like a game of chess, that his father loved to play, the important pieces were all about to fall leading to a clear checkmate and his victory.

He did reveal the loan that Suzanne gave him to resettle Eric. "I'm going to pay her back in full once I've resigned." But he didn't tell her about his arrangement with Alexei. So Simon wasn't really lying to his wife, he was just being very cautious – being judicious with the truth – plus he didn't want any more hand spasms, especially in front in front of Béatrice.

The following day Simon returned to the Embassy not quite sure what to expect. As he entered he was informed that Charles Heyworth wanted to see him. But first of all he dropped by his office to catch up with Stephanie. She smiled when she heard his voice but she looked very nervous when he started asking for updates on all the cultural events the Embassy had been planning. "Are you OK, Steph? You look a bit unhappy? What's been going on?"

"Frankly, Charles is close to having a breakdown. I think he can't cope with all the work. So many staff have been fired or have left that hardly anything is getting done. Thank goodness you're back. Perhaps you can help Charles prioritize tasks. I have had to cancel most the events that you and I planned as I can't get any decisions from him."

"Well, I'm partly to blame as I've been out of the office and was mostly unreachable. But I will go and see Charles now and find out what needs to be done."

What Simon didn't know was that Charles' spouse Anna was pressuring him to make a strong bid to become Ambassador. Unfortunately, she had no clue how these senior appointments were made. She had ignored Charles' long explanations of the process. She treated his rational clarifications as 'excuses for his inability to sell himself to the higher-ups'. In addition, they were both under great stress from the bank who held the mortgage on their gorgeous mansion. The Fontaine family had called in the loan some months ago forcing the Heyworths to refinance with a local bank at a much higher rate. Unfortunately, they had fallen behind in their payments and the bank was threatening foreclosure. "If only you could become Ambassador. That extra $50,000 a year would see us thru and I could keep my family's ancestral home" Anna told him more than once. Charles hated going home at the weekends. He couldn't face her anymore. Instead of returning home he remained at his apartment all weekend gulping away his sorrows into drunken oblivion.

Occasionally, he would find comfort in the arms of another man's wife. They had been having an affair for some time and in Charles' own words 'but for her I would have gone mad'. He really wanted his lover to be with him every weekend; Anna didn't care what he did as she was busy with her interior design projects and socializing with her well-heeled friends at the tennis club. Their children were old enough to take care of themselves. But Charles' amour had to be careful not to arouse her husband's suspicions so their trysts were passionate but short. She had one rule for Charles "you either bury yourself in your booze or you bury yourself in me – your choice". It wasn't a hard decision for him to make although he did whine a lot to her "I can't help drinking, it soothes me. I have a spendthrift wife whose only real love is her f****ing mansion, I hate my job, my son's lover has gone AWOL, the bank is hounding me. Surely just one small drink won't hurt."

"Your choice" his lover repeated. Charles could feel the heat rising in his body; he had never known a woman like her, what she could do with her mouth and her hands was beyond belief. "Either you want these" she said pointing to her firm breasts "or this" picking up a bottle of his favorite liquor. "Let me make it easy for you" she giggled. With one hand she poured the full bottle of liquor into the sink and with the other she lifted her short skirt to reveal her nakedness. "No contest" screamed Charles and he leaped on her.

Sometimes their lovemaking (some may use a different description) took a much different turn. When he was being particularly whining and desperately craving for her body, she would tell him to strip and kneel on the hard floor with his rump up in the air. Knowing what was going to happen next, he would plead with her to be gentle.

"Being gentle is not in my nature. Whiny, ineffective men like you need to be taught a lesson." Next second Charles would hear the swish of the cane.....

Simon found Charles alone in his office. He was sitting back in his chair recalling last weekend's encounter with his lover and dreaming about next weekend's session. He had a silly, lop-sided grin across his face; his hand was caressing a half-full glass of liquor; he appeared to be mumbling some sort of love sonnet to himself. He was surrounded by papers everywhere – it was as if the cold, strong Mistral wind had blown all the way up from the Rhône valley straight into his office. Confidential documents, reports, memos, proposals were all strewn across the floor and the furniture. Charles stopped mumbling and looked up at Simon who had never seen the

Chargé d'Affaires looking so unkempt and haggard. His face was stubbly like cut corn stalks, his eyes were bloated like a frog's and his breathing labored like a dedicated smoker's.

Charles greeted Simon "glad you found time to come to work. Ignore the mess. I'm in the middle of office cleaning."

"I'm here to help. What can I do?" responded Simon ignoring Charles' sarcasm. Simon's encrypted phone pinged and he glanced at the text message. It was a short update from Alexei **'Mission accomplished. $45K sent to Cyprus'**. Simon was relieved that Eric had been removed. Obviously Eric had been very careful with the $100K that Simon had given him. Alexei would be happy with his half of Eric's money. Simon then waited patiently for Charles to answer.

He eventually spoke "I'm off to lunch. Feel free to finish the clean-up." With that he left the office. Simon called in the Ambassador's executive assistant and asked for her help. They both worked on resorting the documents, allocating priorities and drawing up action plans. At 5p Simon asked her to go home as he needed to return to his own office and then visit Charles at his apartment for a heart-to-heart talk. Back in his office he transferred $45K from his Cyprus bank account into the Embassy's transaction ledger as reimbursement for his recent unofficial trips to Hungary and Russia. He then contacted Walter and agreed to meet him for a walk in the Tuileries Garden the following morning. Simon still did not know how he was going to handle the issue with Walter's wife, Mary.

A bleary-eyed Charles opened his apartment door to Simon and asked him in. Entering the lounge, Simon noticed the lingering scent of a strong perfume. It seemed familiar to him but he couldn't place it yet but he knew that one of his female acquaintances used that distinctive fragrance. "Charles, we need to talk. I'm very concerned about you. What's going on?"

A very embarrassed Charles told him about all his troubles – the mansion, the mortgage, his wife's extravagance and expectation, his son Justin's despair and the demands of being Ambassador pro-tem. "It's all too much for me. That's why I'm drinking so heavily. That pleasure and my love for another woman are all that keep my head above water."

Being a diplomat Simon did not inquire into the name of Charles' lover (anyway we're in France!) and instead he talked about the mansion. "Why don't you just sell that huge house and find somewhere else less expensive that you can afford?"

"Sounds easy when you say it like that" Charles responded "but you don't live with someone who drones on and on about her ancestral home, her ancestral heritage. She refuses to sell and move."

"Well if she's that intransigent, why don't you both offer tourists a grand place to stay for their vacations that's in easy reach of all the popular destinations around Paris. I'd recommend you look into Airbnb. She gets to stay and you both get extra cash to help get the bank off your backs."

"Hmm, that's a possibility" Charles replied.

Simon changed the subject. "We should talk about the Embassy and Walter Talbot. What did Walter tell you after I suggested you call him about what I do in addition to cultural affairs?"

"Not much. Since I'm not really the Ambassador, I'm just standing in temporarily, he wasn't able to tell me anything. But I guessed you are working with the CIA on some project. Am I right? Anyway I'm not that concerned about what you do. I'm more focused on getting out of my marriage and living with my lover."

Simon collected his thoughts. "What you do in your private life is really none of my business. But it's all getting a bit complicated. I didn't realize your relationship with Anna was that bad?"

"It would improve if I became Ambassador and brought home lots more cash but I don't see myself being chosen. What do you think?"

"The President will be advised to choose someone else, either another State Department official or someone well-known outside of government service. That's my opinion."

"I agree. In the short term I need your help running the Embassy. I was quite happy being Chargé. Dirty Harry told me what to do and that was fine with me. But now I have to make decisions, read reports, chair meetings, etc. etc. Too much hassle."

"I'm more than willing to help and so is the executive assistant. We'll start early first thing tomorrow morning. How about 7a? I have a short meeting outside the Embassy at 10a. Then next week I have to return for the Purity Committee hearing in DC. When's yours?"

With the first glimmer of a smile he had shown since Simon met him in his office that morning, Charles replied "7a? I'm still sleeping it off then. But I'll make an exception since you're helping me. I think my Senate hearing is next month."

"I'll see you in the office then. Try not to drink too much tonight. The staff are worried about you so it'll be good for them to see you more like your old self."

On the Metro Simon texted his spouse that he would be home soon. He had already decided how he would handle the delicate situation with Walter in the morning. He was looking forward to a quiet evening with Béatrice discussing what they were going to be doing once he had left the Foreign Service.

Next day while Simon was strolling leisurely to the Tuileries Garden for his meeting with Walter, Mary Talbot contacted her sister Amira by phone. Amira had told no-one about her meeting with Simon and Andrew. She was too scared of what Istvan would do to her. But equally she was scared of what would happen to her if he found out. She was worried that once Simon had presented her signed testimony the truth would get out. Although he had promised it would be rated as Secret, she knew that many classified documents had found their way into the public domain thru the Press and WikiLeaks.

When she heard her sister's voice on the phone enquiring whether the big pay-off for her network would be ready for transmission once Simon had been fired by the Purity Committee the following week, Amira was tongue-tied "I'm sorry Mari but I'm suffering from laryngitis. Can't talk much. I'll ask Istvan. I'm sure the $1M will be ready."

"It had better be. I've got a lot of hungry Americans who have put their reputations on the line to bring down Ivan's <u>bête noire</u>, Simon Montfort, also known as Ivan's pain in the ass. I know you and Istvan will be taken care of but I want some assurance that my agents will be rewarded. By the way, one of them is dead. Did you know?"

Amira managed to rasp 'No'.

"Yes, his name was Eric, the guy who worked for Montfort and got fired by the Purity Committee for being gay or whatever. Anyway he was found floating in the Adriatic Sea off the coast of Croatia near Dubrovnik. Weird, right? The local police are saying it was a drowning accident. Tell Istvan I want to have his personal assurance about the $1M or ...."

"Or what?" rasped Amira. "Or I'll go straight to Ivan and he won't be happy. Goodbye little sister."

That one phone call with Mari made Amira vomit all over her lovely Turkish carpets that adorned her beautiful home. She was no longer scared, she was terrified. Had Simon eliminated Eric? Would he be coming after her next?

In the Tuileries Simon walked towards the lanky shape of Walter idling by a park bench as he checked his smartphone. Walter looked up and smiled at Simon saying "I know why you want to see me."

Simon looking very surprised replied "OK, tell me what I'm doing here then."

"It's a long story. It began some years after I asked you to set up a network of agents in Eastern Europe and Russia. Your old girlfriend Amira married Istvan – a good friend of President Ivan of Russia. She mentioned to Istvan that she wanted to find her estranged sister in the US –Mary Weaver, now my wife Mary Talbot. Having found her, Istvan then bribed Mary to become an agent for his intelligence service. Her major task was to bring you down and destroy your network."

Having listened to a version of events slightly different from Amira's testimony, Simon had to sit sat down on the bench for a while. He then looked aghast at Walter saying "I can't believe you did this to me. Amira's postcards, the sting operation on Suzanne, the risks to my family – you allowed all this to take place all the while you knew your wife was making it happen. Why?"

"I suspected my wife but I had no proof. I knew you would get to the bottom of the plot, you are so dogged. In Budapest last week you got the proof, copies of which Andrew sent me. What happened to Suzanne was unfortunate but she's OK and the risks to your family – well I don't believe anyone has been harmed."

"I love your description of my daughter's situation as 'unfortunate'. Sounds a bit like 'collateral damage' when your colleagues in the CIA drop a bomb on an innocent wedding party in Waziristan. So Andrew is CIA? Another fraudster! Now you have written proof of your wife's treachery what are you going to do?"

"Nothing until you have been cleared by the Purity Committee. There's more to this plot than you and I know about. So I'm giving her as much leeway as I can to see what she reveals."

Simon appeared to be seething but realized that Walter did not know or appeared not to know about Charles' affair with Mary. "Is there anything else I should know about Mary – her contacts, her escape routes and so on?"

"No. We are starting 24/7 surveillance on her and we have canceled her passport. We have contacted the Diplomatic Security Service in DC and they are working with the Sûreté to arrest her the day after you've cleared yourself. She will be flown back to the States and formally arraigned on charges of treason, subversion, and conspiracy. She will likely get life without parole."

"Walter, you are so cold about all this. We have known each other for years, in fact you are my closest friend after my wife. You have expressed no sense of remorse for what I'm going thru."

"I always put national security before everything else. If I were in your shoes I would feel very upset, even betrayed, by the way I used you. But in time I hope you will come round and we can be friends again."

"I don't know about that."

Walter walked away knowing that his career was coming to an end. Simon was dumbfounded "I wasn't expecting that. A friend of more than thirty years becomes a traitor in a matter of minutes. He played me for a fool. I shall enjoy my retirement even more when he discovers the full plot."

18 WASHINGTON, DC

Senator Pius read thru the text twice – he and the sender were using a messaging system created by DARPA for the US Intelligence Services. The DARPA texts would self-destruct within 30 seconds of being opened; they would leave no trace on the phone nor on the mobile networks' servers; and lastly the messages could not be reconstituted, even by hackers. The system was the most secure available. Senator Pius was grateful to the political sympathizer in the CIA who gave him access to this useful tool.

The message was short – **Make sure you bury Montfort. Your $500K will be sent immediately we hear that your committee has fired him. This comes from the Top. Don't let us down.**

The Senator swallowed hard and not bothering to acknowledge the message read thru Simon's file one more time. He was a wily former Federal prosecutor who had gained a reputation over the years of getting convictions using debatable interpretations of the law. This is how a fellow prosecutor once described him "he never smiles, he never laughs at a joke and he never cracks a joke. His conversation focuses only on the cases he's handling. His gray hair, his furrowed brow and his unsmiling, mean lips make me think of Fagin in Oliver Twist, but not as generous."

The Senator had told his colleagues that he would be asking all the questions during the Montfort hearing; they were not to interrupt him and in the unlikely event he had left any relevant questions unasked his colleagues were to pass him notes. He wanted to control this hearing to make sure that he got his $500K payoff.

As Senator Pius was working thru his interrogation strategy, Simon was relaxing in Business Class on his way to DC. He was replaying in his mind how he wanted to come over in the hearing. He was expecting it to be hostile as Senator Pius was known for his aggressive style. It was said that he had reduced many defense witnesses to tears when he had been the lead prosecutor in major crime trials.

Béatrice sat next to him reading thru a music score she had composed for a friend of hers in the movie industry. They were talking about the sightseeing they had planned during their short stay when a woman from behind with a very loud Southern accent asked Simon "Is this a first visit to Dee See fir yoo and your pritty littel laydee?"

Glad that they had not been discussing the hearing, Simon winked at his wife, turned round and said "She's not my laydee, she's my lover, thank you." Béatrice looked at her husband and giggled while the Southern woman mumbled "typical rude Yankee." They continued their conversation in French, reasonably confident that the woman from the South would not understand much.

Simon had booked a room at the Capitol Hill Hotel, within walking distance of the Senate. The front desk gave Simon a small Amazon parcel to sign for- Béatrice thought it might be a special book he had ordered. Instead of leaving the testimonies from Eric and Amira in the room safe, Simon asked the hotel manager to put them in the hotel safe for extra security. It was monitored 24/7 by surveillance cameras. (As a precaution Simon had backed up all the evidence onto a thumb drive in an encrypted file he carried with him all the time.) Once they got to their room, Simon opened the parcel and unwrapped a set of three mini pinhole security cameras.

"What are you doing with those?" asked a baffled Béatrice.

"See who comes into our room and checks our stuff. Once we leave our room the cameras will send an alert to my mobile if they have been triggered. I can then view the recording in real time."

"Very James Bond" she laughed.

In the morning they joined a pre-booked hop on/hop off tour group with a guide. The tour was slated to last six hours and included The White House, the Capitol, the Smithsonian and the Lincoln Memorial. As their group was predominantly foreign tourists, they pretended they were French vacationers from Paris. The day began well; the sun was shining and the air smelt fresh despite the heavy traffic. Their coach was spacious and was pleasantly cool. One odd thing struck Simon, though. The tour guide, a young male with an indeterminate American accent (maybe Midwest, thought Simon) kept glancing at them. Simon approached him and with a friendly smile asked "Is there anything wrong? You appear to keep checking on my wife and me."

The guide was embarrassed and said nervously "It's only you said you were from Paris and you don't look like a Parisian."

Simon was taken slightly taken aback by the young man's naïve comment "so what do Parisians look like then? Oh I know – I'm not wearing a black beret, I'm not playing an accordion and garlic bulbs aren't hanging round my neck. Is that the problem?" Simon replied with deep sarcasm.

"Whaaat!" the guide replied. He definitely comes from the Midwest, probably Iowa, thought Simon. That's a typical Iowan response when they want to indicate a total lack of comprehension.

The guide continued "you speak with an American accent. That's what confused me."

Simon replied "uh-huh" and carried on talking to Béatrice.

"What was that all about?" she asked.

"We'll see. Our guide is showing too much interest in us, that's all."

After taking photos of the White House and the Capitol, they were driven to the Smithsonian where they were informed they could stay for 2½ hours. The tourists were encouraged to take a quick lunch at The Courtyard Café. There was so much to see that Simon and Beatrice had wisely planned to visit specific exhibits - the American Indian Museum, the Buddhist exhibit in the Sackler Gallery and the Natural History Museum. Since all that viewing would entail a lot of walking, they would be ready for an enjoyable and relaxing lunch. But as so often happens, their plans didn't exactly work out for them.

Walking to the American Indian Museum, Simon sensed that they were being followed. If you were to ask him how he knew, he would say "I don't know. It's like a ghost taps you gently on the shoulder, you turn round but there's no-one behind you but you then spot a person or a couple behaving out of context. Perhaps it's the way they are dressed, their behavior, their style of walking – it's your sixth sense telling you that something is not right."

He gently took hold of Beatrice's arm and steered her towards a row of display windows, saying quietly to her "act normally, we are being followed. Let's look at the displays and see who is following us in the window reflection. Oh yes, there's our guide talking to someone in a suit. There will be four more of them somewhere, probably two pairs of two. Let's go into the museum and have some fun with them."

"Simon, this isn't my idea of fun. They are going to kidnap us or do something nasty to us."

"Not here they won't. I think they are FBI trainees from Quantico on a surveillance exercise. They are very amateurish. I've just spotted another pair. Here's what we are going to do. I'm going to record what they do and stay on my mobile as we walk towards them."

"You must be stupid."

"We'll be safe. The worst that will happen is a lot expletives from them."

Simon and Beatrice walked towards the group of four, two of whom were talking animatedly on their mobiles.

Simon talked to the youngest-looking trainee and asked him "How are you enjoying the Academy, son? Is SAC Desmond still lecturing there?"

"I don't know, Sir" was the reply. The three other recruits moved away looking very unsure of themselves. Simon moved closer to the young recruit asking "what's your name, son and what's the name of your team leader?"

The FBI trainee responded "Atkins, Sir. And my team lead is Brown."

"Have a good day, Atkins and say hi to your boss for me."

The exchange lasted no more than 12 seconds. Simon whisked Béatrice away towards the exits leaving the recruits totally confused; Simon's mobile beeped and he saw a man in a suit rummaging thru their possessions in their hotel room. It was unlikely he was a hotel employee. They took a cab back to their hotel. By the time they reached the lobby, Simon could see on his mobile that the intruder had already left their room. He asked the manager to give him back all the documents from the hotel safe. In the elevator he checked to make sure they were all intact. By the time they had reached their room, Béatrice's face was bright red.

Before she had a chance to say anything, Simon reassured her "I know, I know, this is not what we planned. The good thing is that they (whoever they are) are only trying to unsettle us and unnerve us before tomorrow's hearing. Don't worry, Béatrice, I'm going to use the security footage from our room and the video recording on my mobile tomorrow morning in front of all the US and International media that will be present. Don't forget all the hearings are live streamed and the audiences have consistently been vast. It's a modern day blood sport – a bit like the gladiators in Roman times, the audience wants to see for themselves who loses and who survives. Well, tomorrow I'm going to survive."

Béatrice was so proud of her husband but asked him to take her back to the airport so she could return home. She didn't feel safe in DC. Simon kissed his wife and said "Of course. I'll take you to the airport and make sure you board safely. Call me when you arrive back home."

They packed everything including the surveillance equipment and left immediately. Simon took his wife back to the airport and she returned to the safety of Paris. He booked into a very modest hotel in Alexandria and planned to arrive at the Senate by train the following morning but first he paid a visit to the Regional FBI offices.

Simon arrived early for the Senate hearing. He had requested to connect his smartphone onto the room's two large screen monitors – one for the Media and the other for the Senators and Simon. At 8a sharp the Media were allowed to enter the room with all their equipment and paraphernalia. Some were allowed to take up position between the Senators and Simon while others had to be content with being placed behind Simon. Anyway the place was full of the traditional as well as the online Press as this particular hearing had been well publicized by the government.

At 9a the three Senators arrived taking their positions on a raised stage so that Simon had to look up at them whether he was seated or standing. Senator Pius sat on a plush chair that was slightly higher than his colleagues' so they had to look up at him. All three looked down on Simon and the Media.

'Great psychology and bad for the neck' thought Simon.

Senator Pius spoke first. He welcomed the Media and introduced himself, his colleagues and Simon. For the record he stated the date and time, mentioning that there would be a 90 minute recess at 12p. He reminded the Media that they were not allowed to interrupt but they could take notes and use their video equipment. Looking down at Simon, the Senator informed him "Mr. Montfort, you are not allowed an attorney or any third party assistance. You are not allowed to plead the Fifth. You have to answer all our questions. Is that clear?"

Simon: Yes it is, Senator. But I should like you to record that I take great exception to these egregious strictures. The Constitution of the USA gives us all specific inalienable rights – rights that can only be removed or changed by Acts of Congress, not by the whim of a President.

Senator: Your objection is noted, Mr. Montfort, but our President has deemed it fitting that these conditions will be followed in accordance with his Executive Order. I'll start the first round of questions. (The Senator was thinking to himself that he had a showboating wannabe lawyer to deal with, not a diplomat. Putting Simon in his place would give him extra pleasure in addition to the $500K.)

Simon: Before you do that, Senator, I'd like to give you, your colleagues and the Media the benefit of seeing for yourselves what happened to me and my spouse on arriving in DC. I'm now running two separate videos – one showing an FBI surveillance team hounding us at the Smithsonian and another showing an FBI agent undertaking an illegal, warrantless search of our possessions at our hotel near here. I showed both videos to SAC Miller at FBI HQ who confirmed the identities of the surveillance team and the intruder in our room. Miller checked with team leader Brown who said 'I was instructed by Senator Pius's office to undertake both assignments utilizing the trainee agents under my command'. Was that part of our President's Executive Order?

Some savvy members of the Media ran outside the stuffy room and started calling their editors alerting them to this strange turn of events. Other Media representatives sniggered and sat dumbstruck waiting for the response.

Senator: Neither am I nor any of my senatorial office are being investigated here today. Mr. Montfort, may I remind you that the purpose of this hearing is to investigate your behavior and your fitness as a Federal employee. Let's proceed.

And so the hearing continued with the Senator asking Simon irrelevant questions about his parents, his education and his time in France as a young man. If the Senator was seeking to unsettle Simon or make him angry, he failed. Simon handled all his questions with a polite directness. When Senator Pius started to talk about his Hungarian girlfriend, the atmosphere changed slightly. He became more aggressive.

Senator: when did you first suspect that your Hungarian girlfriend was a Communist spy?

Simon: that's a loaded question! I never said she was a Communist spy. In fact, she hated Communism and refused to speak Russian. She didn't really want to visit Russia with me. Several members of her family fled Hungry following the 1956 Uprising. Her mother and father were punished. She loathed the Communists.

Senator: all very interesting I'm sure but the fact is that she worked for the Hungarian Trade Delegation – a Communist enterprise.

Simon: that's not accurate Senator. She was employed by the hotel in Chamonix as translator where she assisted a Hungarian Trade Delegation during a conference on the 'Rebirth of Democracy in Europe' in 1988. In the following year Hungary was the first European country to allow the free flow of East Germans into their country so they could reach the free republic of West German. By that time Communism was dead in Eastern Europe.

The Senator realized that he was losing this argument and changed tactics.

Senator: let's move forward to 2021. Why did you raise your daughter Suzanne to be a violent gambling addict?

Simon: another leading question, Senator! Yes, my daughter likes to gamble. Did I or my spouse encourage her to do that? No, we did not. She discovered that she had the knack for gambling all by herself. Is she an addict? No, she's not. In fact, due to an incident in a Monaco casino where she was assaulted, she has given up gambling all together. When you describe Suzanne as 'violent' I assume you are referring to that incident?

Senator: Yes

Simon: Suzanne was provoked to defend herself at the casino. The Monaco police reports are publicly available and they confirm that my daughter was assaulted by a casino security guard. In addition, I have in my possession a testimonial in writing and in video confirming that my daughter was set up by a former US Embassy employee at the behest of a Russian agent code named 'Rita'. The name of this disgraced employee is Eric Haupt, whom this committee fired some months ago. He coerced the son of the Embassy's Chargé to accompany Suzanne and cause the confrontation. It would be illegal for me to disclose the contents of his testimonial in public so I'd recommend that we go thru it in private today.

Senator: this is most unusual. I'll put this request aside until we have completed the hearing. Let's move on, talk about your work as a spy working for the CIA.

The Senator probed into the reasons why Simon agreed to create a network of agents in Europe, what achievements he could share with the committee and how well he knew his CIA handler intimating that he could have been a double agent. Then the Senator switched back to Amira Takács asking a question that got the Media very excited.

Senator: when did you first discover that you had a child by your Hungarian girlfriend?

Simon: you just love these leading questions, don't you Senator. (The Senator sat impassively waiting for Simon's answer). There is no love child, Senator. Again I have documentation in writing and in video denying that we had a child. On this occasion the documentation was witnessed by a senior official at the US Embassy in Budapest. Similar to the previous documents, I'm not able to reveal them in public and would recommend they are reviewed later today in private. The CIA have copies of both sets of documents and have shared them in full with the FBI. They are classified.

Senator: we will reconvene this public hearing once my colleagues and I have examined all your classified documents and videos, Mr. Montfort. You can accompany us to a private room if you so wish.

Simon thought 'if I so wish' – what does he think I'm going to do. Sit here and wait until they issue their findings?

However, before they left the hearing the Senator had one more item to raise.

Senator: there's one small financial matter to discuss, Mr. Montfort. It's a matter of record that you spent a considerable amount of taxpayers' time and money during the last week traveling to Hungary and Russia compiling all these testimonials. Isn't that so? (Simon nodded). You flew business class, stayed in nice hotels, ate and drank well, took up Andrew Weiss' time at the Budapest Embassy and so on. These were not properly authorized business expenses and therefore you have been defrauding the US Government.

Simon: you're absolutely right, they weren't authorized. That was why I transferred US$45,000 into the Embassy account the day after I completed my last trip. I would say that would be enough to cover all my expenses and more.

The Senator had been foiled again. He could see his $500K pay-off slowly disappearing. He pushed his chair back noisily and moved to the private room with his colleagues. As a final attempt to get a guilty plea from Simon, he shoved a single sheet of paper at him. It read:

Charges against Simon Montfort -

Associated with a Communist spy in 1988 and 1989

Had a child out of wedlock with the same Communist spy

Raised his daughter Suzanne to be a violent gambling addict.

Defrauded US Department of State

"I'm reminding you of the severity of these charges. If you are found guilty not only will we fire you, with the loss of your pension rights, but also we can inflict fines and/or prison time on you. These punishments are perfectly legitimate and are in line with the Religious and Moral Purity Act that Congress passed this year. You have one opportunity to save yourself and your family from public humiliation. I do not make this offer very often but in the light of your dedicated public service I'm prepared to make you this offer once only. If you do not accept it now in writing in front of the Committee, then I promise you that we will come down hard on you. You have to admit guilt to all charges and resign immediately.

Understand?

What do you have to say?"

Simon couldn't believe his ears. His reply would have impressed the Roman orator,

Cicero. "Yes, I understand. It is clear to me and to your colleagues, I hope, that you are overreaching your limited powers. My understanding of the Act that Congress passed differs markedly from yours. Firstly, you or your Committee do not have the power to charge me. None of the Committee are Federal prosecutors. Only they have the power to indict. Therefore you can cease using the term 'charges' and use the proper term 'allegations' as instructed by the Act. Secondly, the Act does not refer to any punishments other than termination. I have the Act with me here and I refer you to Section 4 Punishments. Where, Senator, does it mention any other sanction apart from termination? Do you actually think that I'd really come here, with my rights to an attorney and to pleading the Fifth denied, without reading and studying the Act. That is what I have to say. I'd be interested in hearing what your two colleagues have to say – they have been remarkably quiet the whole time."

Senator Pius's fleshy cheeks started to glow a vibrant red and his drinking hand started to shake at the impertinence of this upstart know-it-all. He barked at his colleagues to review the videos and the written documents. After several hours of painstaking clarification from Simon, endless questions from the Committee and constant interruptions from Senator Pius it was time for the Senator to summarize the situation.

He put on his gravelly voice he used always in the Senate to give an air of authority to his pronouncements "I find these testimonials worrisome. They could very well be fake. We would need to question Eric Haupt, your Hungarian girlfriend and Andrew Weiss. While these sessions are underway you will be suspended without pay."

"Again you are overreaching your limited powers. The Act specifically forbids the Committee from interrogating any associates of mine. I am allowed to provide third party testimony. Either the Committee believes it or not. I suspect you have not read the Act – you cannot suspend me with or without pay. I appeal to the two other Senators to speak their minds."

Surprisingly, they did. In fact they both believed Simon's evidence and came very close to apologizing for Senator Pius's 'misunderstanding of the Act'. They voted 1 to 2 to terminate Simon. Senator Pius relayed the decision to the Media with his usual ill-humor. Simon stood on the steps of the Senate for 30 minutes answering all the Media's questions and then hurried away to phone Béatrice saying he was on his way back to Paris. During his phone conversation he confirmed that he would be resigning from the Foreign Service as soon as he arrived back in Paris.

She let him know about some recent news "I've heard from Anna Heyworth that her husband Charles has been put on paid leave due to ill-health. I guess you will have a new temporary boss when you get back."

"Thanks for the update. I've been so busy with the hearing that I haven't had a chance to read all my messages. I'll get to them at the airport. See you soon."

Once Walter heard that his old friend had not been terminated, he gave the go-ahead for the immediate arrest of his spouse – Mary Talbot previously known as Mary Weaver and Mari Takács. She was detained by officers from the Sûreté accompanied by officials from the US Diplomatic Security Service. She was extradited quickly and flown back to DC. Walter then called the Director of the CIA "Mr. Director, in view of my spouse's treasonable acts I have no alternative but to give my resignation with immediate effect. I appreciate you giving me sufficient time to make sure we had enough evidence to arrest and extradite her."

The Director made no objection and wished him well in his next career.

19 MARY TALBOT

Before Mary had been arrested and flown back to the States, she and her sister Amira had been working together very closely to bring down Simon and his network.

Amira was so afraid of Istvan and his threats that she had agreed to help him and his Russian colleagues to undermine and humiliate her former lover. She had managed to reconnect with Mary after a long separation and had asked for her help to undermine Simon reassuring her that she would be well compensated. At the time Amira didn't know that her sister was married to a senior officer in the CIA.

She was cautiously overjoyed when Mary told her – overjoyed because Mary would be able to access information very easily from her husband but cautious as well because her treason might be discovered quickly.

Walter was an experienced counter-surveillance officer and he observed significant changes in his wife's behavior in the prior months. Not knowing what could have happened, he had her phone and computer monitored illegally; he gathered so much information from her conversations with her sister Amira that he was able to get his Director's approval to use Simon as his tool and get evidence that could be used in a court of law in the USA. Walter knew all about the postcards to Simon, the allegations of a love child, the setup of Simon's daughter in Monaco – but chose not to forewarn his good friend of thirty years.

Sitting in her smelly, cold cell Mary Talbot was smiling to herself about her seduction of Charles Heyworth. It had been so easy. He had shared so much about Simon during their post-coital sessions. Like a lamb to the slaughter. All along Charles had been an unwitting accomplice. She hated Simon – she thought he was 'an arrogant little asshole who thinks he knows everything'. She hated the way her husband Walter would go on and on about him – what a great guy, so clever, so knowledgeable. She blamed him for not standing up for Eric and his British lover. (She was very close to the Brit. Although Simon had nothing to do with his demotion, she wanted to blame someone and she chose Simon.) She hated all those boring Embassy dinner parties she had to attend with her husband. So when her little sister asked for her help and promised her a huge reward, she leapt at the opportunity.

Her sister had explained that she was going to send Simon three postcards that would unsettle him and make him worried about his career. "Istvan came up with the idea" Amira said "I was very surprised that he had that much creative ability." (Amira was right to be surprised by her husband as he wasn't that clever; someone else more intelligent and far more devious had suggested the idea to him.)

While in jail the FBI had tried to interrogate Mary several times but she refused to say anything. She even refused to speak to her court-appointed attorney. Charles was in no state to help her. She was left all alone in her cell – she was refusing to eat any food because of her allergies although the jail staff had assured her there were no nuts in the meals. She only wanted water. After 36 hours of solitary confinement she felt unclean, lost and cast aside. She had been allowed to keep two doses of epinephrine. She cradled both injectors in her hand, kept looking at them wondering what she should do. She realized that the prosecution had strong evidence for a conviction of treason, conspiracy and money laundering. She was facing a life term with no parole. The FBI had mentioned a possible plea deal if she released the names of other conspirators like Senator Pius. But she knew she would still have to serve a long prison sentence. Or worse, may be killed for snitching.

So she took the only option that seemed sensible and plunged both injectors straight into her neck. Her blood pressure rocketed causing a massive and fatal heart attack.

20 RUSSIAN CONNECTION

After leaving his Embassy career behind him, Simon suggested to Béatrice they visit London for a short vacation and then stay with his old friend John French and his wife Elizabeth in Birmingham.

"I've kept in touch with him on and off over the past years but I haven't seen either of them since the Berlin Wall incident in 1989. He now runs a nonprofit enterprise and I'd like to catch up with him. What do you say?" Béatrice was in full agreement and they booked flights and reserved accommodation at the Savoy.

The day after they arrived Béatrice opted to spend the morning visiting with some of her friends from the Royal College of Music. They met for an early breakfast at the renowned Fortnum and Mason store in Piccadilly and then visited the many markets that abound in the famous capital city. Meanwhile, Simon was relaxing in their suite looking forward to his full Monty breakfast when the room phone rang.

The front desk announced that 'a Russian gentleman' was waiting for him. "I'll be down in a minute" said Simon. He had been expecting to hear from them and took the elevator to the lobby.

Speaking in hushed Russian his visitor presented his business card confirming he was an Embassy official. "I have a car waiting outside for our drive to the Russian Embassy. President Ivan Ivanovich will be calling you in 60 minutes. Please follow me."

Missing his full Monty, Simon walked to the vehicle and was offered champagne and genuine beluga caviar. Politely declining both, Simon asked for a plate of freshly scrambled eggs with bacon, tomatoes, mushrooms, tea and juice when they arrived at the Embassy. "Certainly" replied his escort.

Arriving at the Russian Embassy located in Kensington Palace Gardens, Simon was swiftly ushered into a special room with all the efficiency that would befit an important visitor. As he enjoyed his hot breakfast, he recalled the very short meeting he had had with the new temporary US Ambassador in Paris.

Simon had requested a private meeting in the Ambassador's office where he handed over his resignation letter and mentioned 'needing to spend more time with my family' and 'I'm sure you will understand that family comes first'. The new temporary Ambassador was a senior official from the State Department and simply took Simon's letter, mumbled a few words of regret and said 'you're probably doing the right thing'. Simon handed over his ID, encrypted phone and credit cards; he was escorted to the front of the building and the Embassy doors were quietly closed behind without another word being said. Now sitting in the Russian Embassy he laughed to himself ironically "an onlooker would think I'd done something wrong, the way the Americans treated me!"

As he finished his solitary meal, his escort re-entered and asked him to pick up the landline as the Russian President was ready.

"Hello Simon. Enjoying your English breakfast? I don't care for that type of food myself – too much fat. Anyway, I wanted to congratulate you personally on a job well done. My brilliant idea of using those three postcards worked out better than I dreamed. You single-handedly brought down the Head of CIA Station in Europe, undermined your own spy network that you had so lovingly created, turned the diplomatic mission in Paris into an absolute mess with a dead Ambassador, an insane Chargé, a fired officer and lastly your resignation. What an achievement! I want to replicate your success in Berlin, London, Rome, Madrid and Lisbon – all those European centers that harbor grudges against Mother Russia. When you leave the Embassy today, Simon, and you check your offshore account in Cyprus you will find the $10,000,000 sitting waiting for you. You earned every cent. I have just one question for you though. What made you betray your country?"

"Firstly, thank you Ivan Ivanovich for your very kind words and for the very prompt payment. I wish I could help you more in your endeavors to extend Russia's influence throughout Europe but I have promised my spouse that my 'diplomatic' life is over. We have a saying in English 'when the writing is on the wall'. I'll explain. It comes from a famous Aramaic saying you will find in Daniel 5 from the Old Testament. For me the political forces in the USA are encouraging our two countries to become close allies. I see no point in working against that trend. So I decided to help you to move the alliance along more quickly. I do have two lingering questions I'd like to ask you. What happened to Amira and to the fifteen terrorist suspects that we identified in Moscow?'

"I too have a lingering question, as you call it, for you. Be assured that Amira is safe. We removed her from Budapest so she wouldn't be harmed by Istvan; she's living near Moscow under an assumed name. Eventually she will join my cyber team in St. Petersburg. She's very clever, you know! Her friend Karik has been recalled and soon they will be able to live together if they want. Next we are going to release the fifteen suspects slowly in small groups without arousing any suspicion. They will be sent to any Islamic country they choose with enough cash to rebuild their lives and keep them quiet. So here's my question for you is – who is your agent in Moscow?"

Simon smiled as he fully expected this question. "Well, Ivan Ivanovich that is the one question I will not answer. All I will tell you is that he is a senior member of your government who does not like you. I don't want him killed. He doesn't deserve it. He has no idea what my real plan was – only you know that. But he believed in me and trusted me." Alexei's daughter's illness wasn't mentioned!

When the President found something very funny he would always let out a hyena-type cackle "you are so serious Simon. I know that at least 20 or more of my senior bureaucrats don't like me. I don't want to kill him. I want to meet him and congratulate him. Eventually I will find out who he is – just kidding you, Simon. I must go. I have to read thru some intelligence documents on your new President for our meeting next week. He has an interesting history and I'm sure I can use some of that against him. Talking about useful people, Senator Pius clearly could not outwit you but he might be useful in the future so I'll keep him around."

The phone went dead. The Embassy official returned, ushered Simon back into the same nondescript sedan and drove him back to the Savoy without saying a word.

During the 40 minute drive Simon had the opportunity to reflect on his actions over the past few months and the conversation with Ivan. He was proud of what he had achieved. He remembered how Walter had divided spies into three groups – the idealists, the greedy and the afraid. He fell into the second group. He was greedy for sure. Also he added a bit of hate into the mix. He had come to loathe most of his Embassy colleagues. How could someone like Dirty Harry be appointed to the post of Ambassador to the French Republic? Most of his peers at the Embassy in Paris looked down on him except for Charles but he was so weak and fearful.

Simon had no sense of remorse for what he had done. Rather he was looking forward to spending a lot of time relaxing with Beatrice and their children. 'I must repay Suzanne when I get back to the hotel'.

21 EPILOGUE

Simon and Béatrice had a great visit with John and Elizabeth. It was a fun and relaxing time for Simon learning about John's charity. He had left Customs and Excise because most of the arrests he made were 'small fry' as he called them. The 'big fish' always got away. So he decided to leave and create his own not-for-profit to fight against human smuggling and sex slavery. It was early days but he had raised several million pounds with promises of more funding in the future. Simon mentioned that he would like to talk more about his organization as he might be able to help.

On the other side of the English Channel life was not so good for Anna Heyworth. Her husband had been declared incompetent by a judge and needed special care. She had him moved to a care home near Paris and she had to sell her beloved mansion and all her precious art at very low prices so she could afford to pay for his 24/7 supervision. Fortunately they had both become French citizens some years before so there was no need to return to the USA.

Unknown to her most of her paintings had been acquired anonymously by Simon thru a third party. They were probably the only aspects of her ancestral home that Simon really liked. They were now stored securely in a vault in Cyprus.

The Heyworth's son Justin had lost the love of his life, Eric, and now he had lost his father to early dementia; he and his mother Anna decided to rent an apartment from where she could continue to run her business and where Justin could write and publish his novels of romantic love under the pseudonym of Suzanne Sagan.

Simon was starting to feel the effects of the treachery that he had undertaken. At nighttime when he was in a deep sleep, his active subconscious started to work overtime. Apparitions of all of the people he had wronged accused him of deception, greed, conspiracy, selfishness and murder. The faces of his wife, his children, Amira, Eric, Charles and Walter appeared night after night causing him to wake with his blood pounding in his head and his body covered in the sweat of his guilt. On the worst nights the cruel face of Ivan Ivanovich joined the line of accusers saying "I know what you really are, I know what you've done. I control your life now."

Béatrice became very worried about Simon. He tried to minimize her concerns saying it was just a passing phase. But it wasn't and it wouldn't be..... His parents had passed onto him their skills of illusion and language and now he would have to live with the consequences of his choices for the rest of his life. Much like the artists and painters that he had seen and adored in his youth, he had created his own version of Illusionism – an art form mastered by the famous Salvador Dali.

On the one hand Simon had persuaded family, friends and co-workers into believing what he said and what he did while at the same time 'with the other hand' like a magician he had destroyed careers, betrayed his country and aided Russian expansionism.

ABOUT THIS BOOK

The Diplomatic Spy (Simon Montfort Series Book 1)

Deception***Greed***Illusion***Jealousy***Murder***Treachery

Against the backdrop of the Berlin Wall and Russia's resurgence following the collapse of the Soviet Empire, we witness the rise of Simon Montfort's career to a senior diplomat position at the US Embassy in Paris. As Simon's career develops, one of his oldest friends recruits him as a spy for the CIA. He agrees to help the CIA gather 'intel' on Russia's expansionist plans and assist the Agency to undermine the Kremlin leadership in Moscow. Simon creates a network of agents in Budapest, Istanbul, Moscow, Vienna, Sofia and other East European cities.

 After several years of success where his network has employed cunning surveillance techniques to weaken the security of the Russian President, Simon is suddenly plunged into a many-sided struggle – the election of a nationalistic, pro-Russian and extremely religious government in the USA, the subtle threats from a former lover, the powerful forces of a new expansionist Russian empire and the loving expectations of his loyal family – they all conspire to test his ability and his allegiances. His moral code is at stake. Be prepared for clever illusion and cold-hearted treachery.

ABOUT THE SERIES

This is Book 1 of 3 in the Simon Montfort Series.

Book 2 will be published late 2020.

ABOUT THE AUTHOR

Shawn Callon immigrated to the USA from Europe in 1994. The Diplomatic Spy is his first novel in the Simon Montfort Series, in fact this is his debut novel. His interest in politics and spying comes from his extensive international travels in Africa, Asia, Europe and Latin America where he worked with government institutions and large commercial operations. He loves reading fiction and particularly enjoys John Le Carré's novel. Shawn describes his admiration for Le Carré " I love the complexity of his work and the 'greyness' of his major characters. His 'heroes' aren't tall, dark and square-jawed; they can be rather unhealthy and plump or drunks or just plain failures. He is the modern fiction writer that I admire most and would say he is the best in his modern genre."

Shawn lives in the Midwest with his spouse, Elizabeth, who worked tirelessly as his editor helping him to identify grammatical errors and stylistic inconsistencies and contributing to the overall development of the book.

Shawn Callon is a pseudonym. The novelist welcomes your comments directly and he will do his best to respond to you promptly.

You can reach him by emailing shawncallon@gmail.com.

CPSIA information can be obtained
at www.ICGtesting.com
Printed in the USA
LVHW040927181119
637663LV00006B/2501